# SHILLING & FLORIN

## BOOK ONE:
### THE JACK OF HEARTS MURDERS

# KATE HALEY

*To all my friends who make cameos in this series.*
*I'm so sorry…*
*but only like five of you will read this,*
*so I'm probably safe.*

# CONTENTS

Visit **www.katehaleyauthor.com** for
deals and current news from the author.

# 1

The night was dark and cold. A gentle mist was creeping through the streets like the fingers of misbegotten ghosts. The tall streetlamps down this side of the park had yet to be lit. Faint moonlight glinted off the wrought iron fence, illuminating the spiked tips like a legion of spears in the night. It lasted a moment, then the light vanished behind the clouds. The darkness was pervasive along the spooky old path. Brown leaves gathered in clumps near every available windbreak, as though huddling out of the cold.

No one heard the scream. It was muffled and cut abruptly short. The wind stirred and all the leaves danced. The sounds of their revelry drowned out any meek human noises. When their party subsided, a faint panting could be heard and the tiniest clink of glass on stone. No one was listening. The breeze started up the festivity again and the world continued to ignore whatever was happening in the shadow of the trees.

It was half an hour before the lamps were lit and anyone knew anything had happened at all.

When dawn broke it was weak and watery and not enough to rouse Charles Shilling from his agitated sleep. That took the bang and rattle of the cell door as the bars were slid back. He startled, half falling from the bench he was sleeping on, and staggered to catch himself. One hand latched onto the slatted seat, holding him up before more than his shoes hit the floor. He eased himself back onto the bench with a groan, this time sitting upright.

"Rise and shine, Mister Shilling!" a voice called to him.

Charlie groaned again and rubbed his face like he could force life into it. His gloved fingers were cold. Everything was cold, dear God, so cold. He staggered to his feet, ruffling his hair, and grabbing the coat he had been using as a pillow. He shook it out from its rolled-up state and slung it on, shivering in the depths and wondering if he would, in fact, have been better served wearing it than sleeping on it last night. The question had been a topic of some contention between the two halves of his brain in the previous darker hours.

He looked up, bleary-eyed, to see two uniformed officers watching him from the doorway. He recognised them from last night. The brunette man and blonde woman who had arrested him. Constables, by the uniform. They looked about as happy as he did. He squinted at the tiny crack of barred window, glimpsing more of the morning than he could bear.

"It took you idiots all night to find someone who could verify me?" he grumbled, stumbling towards the doorway.

"No one verified you, Shilling," brunette male constable said. "But orders made it down. Lord Pound wants to see you."

"Eh, well, tell him I haven't found anything yet because two idiots arrested me last night," he retorted.

"You'll have to tell him yourself, Mister Shilling," blonde lady constable insisted.

Charlie stopped. The officers were not overly tall people, but neither was he, and they were standing very resolutely in his way. If things were about to get rough, he could probably take them, but he didn't like fighting unless he absolutely had to. Besides, they had truncheons, and he had already had a very bad night. He was already in jail, and hitting police would not get him released in a hurry. Of course, it was starting to feel like not hitting police hadn't gotten him released in a hurry either. These two, dense as they might have been, looked firm and awake. Charlie was neither.

"Now?!" Charlie groaned. "He wants to see me right now?!"

"We have been instructed to escort you to his residence," blonde lady constable assured.

Charlie didn't find it assuring at all. He poked his tongue around his mouth. It was dry and disgusting and tasted like soap lather. His face was cold and greasy, and his hair felt like it was mostly on end.

"Could I maybe have a cup of tea first...?" he inquired hopefully.

"Now, Shilling," brunette gent constable insisted, firmly guiding Charlie from the cell.

The Pound household was aflutter with activity. The party wasn't until tomorrow, but preparations were already beginning. Amelia Florin, adopted Pound and fairly-soon-to-be wedded Pound, flounced down the stairs to the dining room. It was a large, well-lit space in keeping with the rest of the mansion. The long, polished mahogany table shone, and the highbacked chairs were arranged precisely about it. She swooshed into the room in a flurry of dark burgundy skirts.

Lord Henry Pound was sitting at the head of the table, deep in his newspaper, his breakfast growing cold and forgotten. Beside him sat his grown son Harry, who was meticulously applying spreads to his toast. Harry looked up as she came in and threw her a winning smile, which she returned openly.

"Amy, stop flouncing," Henry ordered without surfacing from his newspaper.

"Sorry, Daddy," she apologised, falling into an even step as she approached the table.

"Oh, let her flounce, Dad," Harry protested. "She graduates tomorrow, she's allowed to be excited."

"Unseemly for a doctor to flounce," Henry huffed.

Harry looked up at her as she approached and mouthed 'flounce away'. She chuckled, wandering to him at a measured pace. He motioned to her and she offered her hand. He kissed it. She brushed his chocolate brown fringe from his face and kissed the top of his hair. Henry folded his paper down to glare at them.

"At the dining table!" he exclaimed in exasperation.

"Would you rather we take it somewhere else?" Harry asked pointedly, ignoring Amy's warning slap on his shoulder.

"Don't be vulgar, boy," Henry warned. "I raised you better than that."

The Lord of the Manor lifted his prominent nose high, and his paper higher, hiding his face. Well, most of it. He had sideburns large enough to shame whole proud species of the animal kingdom, and even in the depths of the newspaper his whiskers marked his presence.

Amy pulled up a chair next to Harry as he carefully quartered his toast. The maid brought her tea and she settled down, declining the gestured offer to share in her fiancé's toast.

The knock at the door came mere seconds later, and the butler appeared in the doorway.

"My Lord," he began, "Constables Bond and Wilson are here to see you, along with Mister Shilling."

"Thank you, Digby," Henry sighed, folding away his paper. "Show them in."

Digby bowed and left the room.

"Father, you're not letting that wretched creature in the house, are you?" Harry exclaimed.

Amy saw a quarter of the front page as the paper was set on the table. She quickly filled in the blanks to complete the headline and her heart sank.

"Not again…" she sighed.

"Exactly, Amy," Harry rested a hand on her arm in

agreement. "Not at the breakfast table."

"No, Harry," Amy pointed at the paper. "There's been another one. That makes… what? Fifteen in the last year?"

"And two just in the last week," Shilling grumbled from the doorway.

Everyone looked to him. Digby stood stiffly in the doorway with Shilling at his shoulder. Charles was the same age as Harry, but Amy couldn't imagine two people more different. Harry sat straight-backed and impeccably dressed in his chair, a look of utter disdain on his face. Shilling, on the other hand, all but ignored him. His straw-stack blonde hair was scruffy, his long tan coat was rumpled, and his suit looked like he'd slept in it — it didn't look like it had been a good sleep. He only had eyes for the head of the table.

"You wanted to see me, Lord Pound?" he huffed.

"Hello Shilling," Henry smiled at him. "I hear you got yourself in a spot of trouble last night."

"It's not my fault the police are morons," Shilling grumbled.

"I wouldn't call London's Finest 'morons'," Harry sniped.

Shilling cocked his head to the side and regarded Harry with exhausted exasperation. His brows furrowed and his eyes squinted.

"Mister Shilling, you look awful," Amy began, heading off further disagreement. "Would you care to take a seat?" She indicated across from her.

Shilling slouched into the room and sat down opposite Harry, on Henry's other side.

"Can we get you anything?" Amy continued.

"Tea...?" he answered in a small, hopeful voice.

"Penny, could you please...?" Amy turned to the maid.

"Already on it, Miss," Penny replied politely, setting tea in front of their guest and pouring it out. Shilling looked up at her with adoring eyes.

"Thank you, Miss. You're an angel," he told her gratefully.

Penny gave the dishevelled young man a shy smile. As she stepped back, Shilling drained his cup. It barely touched the sides. Penny came back and refilled the mug. She stayed nervously attentive this time, but Shilling was already regarding Lord Pound. Henry's thick grey eyebrows were narrowed at the young man at his table.

"I hear you were caught red-handed last night," Pound commented.

"Hardly!" Shilling protested. "There might have been a body, but I'm not exactly the type to stick my hands in the mess."

"He doesn't mean you had actual blood on your hands, lunatic," Harry sighed. He glared across the table. "They think you're the Jack of Hearts?"

"I was accused and charged last night," Shilling admitted.

"And you're not still locked up because...?" Harry demanded.

"Because I didn't do it," Shilling replied. "And I can't believe it took them all night to verify that! I told them! Ask anyone! Detective Rupee is working the case, she knows I'm not the killer. I told them to contact my sisters, or Commissioner Farthing, or Captain Hedley, anyone from up in the northern precinct, even Madam Bronny!"

"It's okay, Shilling," Henry soothed. "No one thinks you did it."

"Speak for yourself, father," Harry commented. He folded his napkin over his plate and stood, tracing the tips of his fingers lovingly against Amy's back. "Fortunately, I have pressing business away from the discussion of this gruesome ordeal."

"You running away from me, Henry Junior?" Shilling raised an eyebrow.

"From you, Shilling? Never," Harry retorted. "That's a fight I could win with my eyes closed. But the law calls... you know, the right side of it."

"With a tongue that sharp I'm surprised you're not a better litigator," Shilling quipped.

"Shilling!" Henry snapped.

"I'm serious," Shilling insisted, deadpan. "I've seen some of his cases. I could prosecute more successfully than him and I don't believe in incarceration."

"Luckily for the world, Mister Shilling, it believes in you," Harry finished. He kissed Amy's cheek and strode from the room. She watched him go, hoping he wasn't too flustered. He might have presented a cutting exterior, but she knew how easily things got under his skin.

Shilling, on the other hand, sat there in his rumpled coat sipping his tea like he was accused of murder most evenings.

"It is possible, Mister Shilling," Amy began slowly, "that if you weren't so rude to people, they wouldn't arrest you and leave you in a cell all night, only to let the Commissioner know you'd been arrested in the morning."

The young man's eyes narrowed and his lips pursed as he considered this.

"I was just being honest..." he explained.

"Yes, Shilling," Henry sighed. "Your honesty is infamously brutal. Now, what have you found?"

"Not as much as I'd like," Shilling admitted, sitting his cup carefully in its saucer. "Like I said, last night was frightfully bungled. When word went out that they'd found another body, I got the message before the police. So, naturally, I got to the scene before they did. I was able to investigate a bit, but it wasn't long before I was in cuffs and they were trampling over everything."

"The paper says it's Jenny Kent." Henry tapped it with a finger. "She's another one of Bronny's girls. That's her seventh. Nearly half of these killings have been from her House."

"That sounds about right," Shilling nodded. "I know she's scared. That's why she's hired me."

"*We've* hired you, Shilling," Henry insisted. "The city has hired you to help with this."

"Begging your pardon, Lord Chief Justice, you didn't hire me. You dragged me into your office one day and told me to solve it, after Bronny had already asked for my help because Farthing and his buffoons had let eight women die."

"Don't pretend you weren't poking around before

that, boy," Henry warned. "I know you were snooping. I heard the enraged screams from the lead detective."

Shilling pursed his lips again, contemplating his cup and silently tapping his fingers either side of the rim. He didn't know Rupee well, but he did recall her screaming at him once.

"Eight women were dead, I was intrigued..." he admitted softly.

"But it's not just that, is it?" Amy asked, joining the conversation and settling back with her tea. "They didn't just die, gentlemen, they had their hearts brutally cut out. The Jack of Hearts has specifically targeted expensive, high-class consorts from notable families who will want him brought to justice."

"Well, we don't know that he's actively targeting the ladies," Henry sighed. "No one has mentioned anything untoward in their lives before the incidents."

"I think we can be fairly confident, Lord Pound," Shilling commented, still tapping his cup. "Our killer hasn't targeted any of the men from the same establishments, only women, always after dark — and yet, we haven't found ourselves with any dissected doctors or bakers or cleaners on our hands. Always escorts who took a job outside one of the High Houses and were supposedly returning from it."

"Fine, good," Henry encouraged. "So how is he picking them? Why is he picking them? Come on, Shilling! You said you'd sort this seven bodies ago! I cannot have another paper like this on my doorstep and another set of grieving parents demanding to know why the city isn't safe for their little girl to get work experience!"

"If I had the answers, Henry, we wouldn't be in this pickle," Shilling grumbled, rubbing his face.

Amy raised an eyebrow at him, but he had his hands over his eyes and didn't see. She was glad Harry wasn't still here. He probably would have smacked Shilling for talking to his father like that.

"The deeply disturbing psychology behind a man killing these women is all very compelling," Shilling sighed wearily, pinching the bridge of his nose. "There are half a dozen decent theories, and I don't have any faith in a single one." He took a deep breath, rubbed his eyes, and looked up at them. "I know my work on this hasn't been good enough, but I swear I'm doing my best. There just isn't enough evidence. Whoever is responsible for these deaths is a butcher with a knife, but a meticulous worker. They are targeting specific women, stealing their hearts, and I cannot work out what links the ladies aside from their work. It keeps coming back to that, and I have scraped the streets for motive — we've had over ninety suspects! None of them are butchering ladies."

"Then whatever it is, is happening in an area you're not looking," Amy commented.

"I'm very aware, Miss Florin," Shilling sighed. He paused abruptly and cocked his head to the side, regarding her. It was a very puppy-dog gesture.

"Charlie…?" Henry warned, also noting the look.

"Miss Florin? Are you still Miss Florin, or did you finish pursuing medicine?" Shilling inquired curiously.

Amy smiled at him over the rim of her mug.

"I'm surprised you even remember Daddy telling you about my exploits," she said.

"I don't forget things," Shilling replied.

Amy's smiled widened. She couldn't help herself. She didn't know Shilling well, but she knew him well enough to know he didn't brag. The police didn't like him because he came across as arrogant, but he had sway with the nobility because he was effective. His statements, although far from politely modest, were always true. Charles Shilling didn't forget things. He was too brilliant for that.

"I did finish pursuing medicine," she answered finally. "I graduate tomorrow. Tomorrow afternoon, you will be looking at Doctor Florin."

"Only if I see you tomorrow afternoon," Shilling replied. "Congratulations on your accomplishment."

"Thank you," she preened.

"Are you moving into work?"

"Not immediately. I have options, but Harry and I haven't set a date for our wedding yet, and that might take precedence," she answered.

"Hm," Shilling nodded. "Miss Florin, I don't suppose I could trouble you for your aid in this investigation?"

"You what?" Henry coughed.

"I have been contemplating the need for an independent medical examiner," Shilling elaborated. "Someone separate from the police, and you are currently independent of all hospitals. Also, I want a woman's opinion on these murders."

"You want a woman's opinion?" Amy smiled,

raising an eyebrow at him.

He nodded earnestly at her. "With the exception of one mortician who is either an imbecile or corrupt, all the doctors I've spoken to so far have been men, which I see as a complete lack of insight on behalf of the department, given that the victims have all been women. Last week I raised a theory that the killer might be a woman, and they nearly laughed me out of the office." A small frown of confusion pouted his bottom lip ever so slightly. "Which doesn't make any sense."

"Statistically speaking the killer is more likely to be male," Amy offered.

"Maybe," Shilling sipped his tea. "But I've been over every man with ties to the High Houses in London and I'm coming up dry. Our killer is getting bolder — they know we've got nothing. I think it is at least worth investigating, and someone with medical training and an eye for things I won't see would be extremely useful. Pound here can get us permission." He nodded his head at Henry.

Amy looked at her surrogate father, who was already bristling with indignation.

"All right," she replied quickly, taking the wind out of the Lord's sails.

"All right?" Henry echoed. "Amy, are you sure?"

"Daddy, if there's anything I can do to help stop these brutal killings, I should at least try," she insisted. "I know I'm a junior doctor at best, but if Shilling thinks I can help, it would be deeply remiss not to even have a look."

Shilling raised his eyebrows as high as they would

go in Henry's direction. The older man saw the look and sighed. He probably would have been more supportive of Amy's decision if they hadn't been sharing the table with Trouble and his articulate facial expressions. Charlie Shilling had crooked eyebrows and a crooked nose and a crooked smile that all seemed to ask, 'what's the worst that could happen?' No one ever wanted to know the answer.

"Very well," Henry conceded. "I shall draft a message to the morgue. Shilling, can we interest you in some breakfast before you start work?"

"No, thank you, Pound," Shilling shook his head. "I was actually thinking I might briefly duck home. Miss Florin, I could meet you at the morgue at, say," he checked the cracked and chipped watch in his pocket, "ten-thirty?"

"That would work perfectly," Amy agreed. "I was supposed to meet the ladies at ten, so I can stop by fleetingly on my way instead of sending apologies."

"Then I will meet you there," Shilling replied, dismissing himself and standing from the table.

No one said anything as he left abruptly. Henry closed his eyes and shook his head gently, as though willing God to give him strength. The help all gave Shilling a wide berth and varied looks. Amy tried not to laugh. She couldn't hide her grin, but she knew he wouldn't have noticed. He never noticed the strange looks everyone gave him everywhere he went, and he would have no idea they all considered his departure abrupt. He had places to be and things to do and heavens only knew why everyone else dallied so slowly.

"I'm glad you find it so amusing…" Henry sighed.

"Oh, come now, Daddy," Amy smiled. "He's a harmless wee fruitcake."

"No, he isn't," Henry warned. "But I know what you mean. Shilling means well, Amy. He means very well. Boy has the best of intentions, but he's a few cards short of a full deck, and he moves through life like a hurricane. I know I don't need to warn you not to get caught in his storm."

"You don't," Amy assured, standing and coming around the table to kiss his cheek. "Don't worry, Daddy, I can handle Charles Shilling."

"Excellent," Henry grumbled. "I should give you my job then."

Amy laughed at him. He kissed her cheek in return and gave her a pat on the shoulder before turning his troubled frown back to the newspaper. He left it folded up but tucked it under his arm as he departed the table and headed for his study.

# 2

It wasn't far from the Pound's Mayfair home to Charlie's house, but he hurried anyway. There was much to do, so much, and it needed to be done six months ago. Last night was the earliest he'd ever made it to the scene of one of the Jack's crimes. It had been his best chance to see things as fresh as possible, and it had been bungled. Time was making the wounds worse. The faces of all the dead women he'd failed to save were starting to haunt him. He was supposed to be better than this. It just didn't make any sense.

His feet trailed themselves down Kensington, past the museum, hurrying distractedly through the world. It wasn't until the smell of the bakery hit his nose that his brain rebooted. Charlie had few things he loved in his life. He had a deep passion for his work and anything that could make him think deeply. He loved his sister, and he supposed by extension his sister-in-law, although given the nature of siblings that sometimes felt more like an obligation. He could count his friends on one hand, in fact he barely needed two digits. But he loved bread. He was fairly certain that what he felt for bread was love, insomuch as love was something he felt. That love of bread, and the ear to the ground that the bakery boys kept, had led to the closest thing Charlie had to friends.

The Pence Bakery was directly opposite his house. He could see it from his bedroom window. Many a morning was begun with a trip across the road for news from the street and a fresh pastry. Today that walk had taken significantly longer. Luckily, the bakery was between crowds. It was moderately busy, but not so much that Charlie couldn't slip through the door and dodge the queue.

The bakery was a dinky wooden shop filled with bread baskets and that heavenly, warm, yeasty scent. Just the hot smell alone eased some of the kinks Charlie had picked up sleeping on the bench. Front of house was run by Terry, the oldest of the Pence siblings. He was the most personable, with the loudest voice, and could usually keep the rest of his siblings in check. He saw Charlie sneak in behind the cluster of customers and a grin split his face instantly. He turned to the hole in the wall behind him.

"Michael!" Terry called into the bakery at the back. "You're up."

A slight, dark-blonde man, heavily dusted with flour, staggered out of the kitchen. Charlie ducked behind the counter and followed the baker out the side door. Michael held the door open as Charlie followed him out. They shared an exhausted nod as they stumbled into the alley together. Michael handed over a freshly baked butter-washed knot. Charlie fumbled for his wallet but Michael laughed him off.

"On the house," he offered, pressing the bread into

Charlie's hands. "I hear you spent the night in the clink. We were worried when you were late this morning, after the rumours last night."

"It would take more than that to get rid of me," Charlie muttered, ripping a lump off the knot and stuffing it in his mouth. The crust was buttery and crunchy, and the inside was light and fluffy. It was heaven.

"You're chasing a serial killer," Michael pointed out.

Charlie gave that comment a conceding nod, chewing his bread. "Haven't come close to catching them though," he admitted, ripping off another corner to munch.

"That you know of," Michael countered. "I know you, Charlie. You might be closer than you think."

Charlie pulled a face. The point was sound. It was entirely possible the Jack of Hearts had been in his sights before and he'd missed them. That almost made it worse. Something was missing though. It shouldn't be this hard. The problem was a complete lack of motive. Even when he whittled it down to the concept that someone just liked collecting human hearts, it didn't fit all the strange holes of the case. It took a particular kind of person to commit such gruesome acts, and the usual suspects had all been dead ends.

"What's the word this morning?" Charlie asked, before shoving more bread in his face.

"Bronny's ropable," Michael grimaced. "All the Madams are. They've started laying down hard rules. None of the ladies are allowed out in groups smaller than three, even during the day. Most groups must be chaperoned by a man unless they're staying extremely public. Lot of the girls have started carrying weapons under their skirts, just in case."

"That's no way to live," Charlie disapproved, mouth full.

"You're telling me," Michael agreed, fishing another bread knot out of his pocket and handing it over. Charlie took it gratefully. This time he waited until he'd swallowed before speaking.

"I'll stop by to see Bronny later. First thing this morning I'm heading to the morgue with Amelia Florin to see what we can uncover about Jenny's death."

Michael raised an eyebrow.

"Florin?" Charlie supplied. "Medical trainee. Lord Pound's adopted girl."

"That's all names above my social class," Michael smiled.

"No one's above your social class, Mike," Charlie insisted, still ripping and snacking.

Michael grinned. "I know you've got opinions on all this, Charlie, but society disagrees with you, and I ain't tangling with no Lord nor his daughter. She sounds learned, so good for her. Hope she can help you."

"I hope so too," Charlie sighed. His eyes narrowed in contemplation as he nibbled ripped titbits of bread. "She's an interesting fish, Miss Florin."

"An interesting fish?" Michael chuckled.

Charlie nodded. Michael folded his arms and leant back against the wall.

"All right, I'll bite," he admitted.

"She's just another figure to further reinforce my

point that blue blood is a myth, and the lies of the wealthy are designed to further a system of oppression implemented by the nobility to keep themselves in power by manipulating basic human instincts," Charlie huffed.

"If this is the part where you climb on your soapbox, Charles, and start screaming 'down with the monarchy' again, I'm going inside," Michael grinned.

"You should be supporting me," Charlie argued.

"I do, Charlie," Michael smiled. "We all do. We just worry about you. You do a lot of anti-monarchist yelling for a member of the nobility."

"No, no I'm not," Charlie pointed at him warningly, mouth and hands still distracted by bread. "My sister married into it and dragged me along with her, there's a difference. You could get there the same way I did — same way Florin did."

"Did her sister marry a noble too?"

"Her mother," Charlie answered. "Lord Pound's younger brother, idiot Pound junior, showed up on his brother's doorstep one day with a new pregnant wife. That woman was a lady most well-known as Elizabeth Florin."

"Most well-known?" Michael raised an eyebrow.

"Con-woman," Charlie smiled. "Genius. No one knows her real name. She drained Pound junior of his wealth, had the child — which they abruptly discovered wasn't his — and vanished into the night, leaving her latest husband to have a complete mental breakdown."

"How did they know the kid wasn't his?" Michael asked.

"Lizzie Florin has red hair, pale skin, and freckles, and the Pounds are all very English Rose," Charlie answered.

"The daughter's black?" Michael checked.

"More like walnut," Charlie commented, shoving more bread in his mouth. "She looks a lot like her mother — same burgundy curls and green eyes, but dark skin with darker freckles. Clearly not a Pound. Yet, Lord Henry took her in. He'd lost his own wife a year before, had his baby son to deal with, his younger brother had to be committed to protect himself, the mother was gone, and he said none of that was the baby's fault. Couldn't send her off somewhere else. Took her in and betrothed her to his infant son. Obviously, there are some dubious aspects to the whole thing, but I always respected him a little more once I learnt what he'd done."

"When did this happen?" Michael asked.

"About... twenty years ago?" Charlie shrugged, scoffing the last of the bread.

"So why do you know about it?" Michael pressed. "You would have been a baby, if that."

"Looked into the case once," Charlie answered. "Was curious. Did some digging on Pound in case it could be useful. Also, Lizzie Florin was interesting. No one knew what happened to her. Disappeared like smoke."

"Where is she?" Michael grinned.

"Went up to Scotland first and bailed to Germany a few years later," Charlie shrugged. "Wasn't that hard to follow. Figured it was worth investigating in case

Pound ever wanted to know."

Michael was still grinning at him.

"The important thing is that both Florin women appear encouragingly bright, and have no noble birth to claim, much like myself, and you, of course —"

"Don't drag me into this, Charlie," Michael protested, raising his hands defensively.

"You couldn't run the word on the street like you do without some nous," Charlie grinned at him.

Michael grinned back, but he declined to comment. He just scratched his cheek and failed to look innocent. The sass of it deepened Charlie's grin. He brushed his hands on his coat and dug out his wallet again, tipping a few coins into his hand. Michael tried to protest, but this time Charlie waved him off.

"It's for the information, not the food," he lied, pressing too many coins into his friend's hands. "Hate to love you and leave you, but I have a sister to fight with and a serial killer to catch."

"Just another day in the kitchen for you, huh?" Michael drawled. He clinked the coins in his palm with a wry smirk. "You're an utter rascal, Charlie Shilling."

"Takes one to know one," Charlie clapped him on the shoulder and then ducked away down the alley. It was a shame he didn't have more time to spend, but they were both busy. Still, Charlie appreciated having someone in his life who was the same brand of socially awkward as him. Mike definitely fit that mould, which made him excellent company when he wasn't elbows deep in flour. Not that Charlie could talk, presently elbows deep in bodies — metaphorically speaking.

He dashed across the road, skipped up the steps, and through the front door. Any attempt at a quiet entry was thwarted by the Butler. Charlie did not believe in nemeses, but Jasper Quid (a.k.a. The Butler) disagreed with Charlie about a great many things, including things Charlie didn't think they should disagree on and didn't understand why they disagreed about them, and now seemed to take a perverse delight in tormenting him.

The front door opened into a towering cart of unbalanced silverware. There was no way to avoid it, even if Charlie had been expecting it. He realised, as he stood in the clanging wreckage, that he should have expected it, and blamed his surprise on the intense distraction of murder. Jasper poked his head into the entrance hall from a nearby room, a malicious grin of cunning plastered across his face.

"It lives," he declared as the clatter subsided.

Charlie stood with the door wide open, the punted cart and an array of silverware at his feet.

"Really, Jasper?" Charlie sighed, shoving his way in and closing the door behind him. "How could you possibly think blocking the door was a good idea?"

"It wasn't blocked, sir, and everyone else was accounted for," Jasper replied. "Lady Rebecca has been most worried about you."

"Charlie!" A mighty bellow drifted down the stairs.

Charlie sighed. He hurriedly gathered the scattered silverware.

"Please, Master Shilling," Jasper bid him, trying to wave him off. "There's no need for that, sir. I'll have a maid collect it."

"You will not. Your pranks are not their problem." Charlie glared at him and clanked the silver back on the trolley. "Abolish the aristocracy!" he declared heatedly in Jasper's face, before storming up the stairs. He made it up to the first floor just as his sister Rebecca was sweeping down to find him. He hurried for the door to his room, but it was too late. She'd seen him. Not that she wouldn't have been able to find him easily anyway.

"Charlie!" she yelled, chasing him into the bedroom. "Prison, Charlie? Really?! Prison?!"

"Jail, technically," he corrected, shrugging out of his coat and tossing it on the neatly made and clearly unslept in bed. God, it looked so inviting… but there was no time. No time for comfortable things. He ducked behind the folding screen where his wash basin stood, still stripping off clothes as he went.

"Don't be a smart-arse, Charles," Rebecca scolded him. He could hear her pacing irritably on the other side of the screen. "I know you're hunting that serial killer, after I told you not to! How did you get yourself locked up? Which poor officer did you mortally offend?"

"I didn't offend anyone," Charlie huffed. The water in the basin was clean but cold as he hurriedly scrubbed himself down with a washcloth. "They were just being obtuse."

The silence of Rebecca's disbelieving eyeroll was profound. He could hear it through his splashing. It was accompanied by a series of footsteps. More people. Couldn't a newly freed man have a wash in peace? Was it so much to ask?

"What happened, Charles?" a new voice called to him. There was an expectation of obedience in that voice, Charlie had always found. Lady Susan Guinea gave orders, and they were carried out. Always. Charlie both begrudged and admired his sister's wife for that. He did not like her titles, but he had accepted that they were not the only reason people listened to her. Susan had gravitas. Charlie knew with tragic certainty and profound jealousy that he did not.

"I was trying to keep them from contaminating the crime scene last night," Charlie huffed. "I got there first and then the police came and started trampling everywhere and making a mess. I needed them out of the way, and I told them to keep back, and they started making a ruckus before deciding I was a threat and possible killer, whereupon they arrested me."

"Oh Charlie…" Rebecca sighed in exasperation.

"They didn't even bother to verify anything I told them until morning," he grumbled. "How do you two even know about it?"

"The cute boy from the bakery across the road kindly informed us," Susan told him.

"Which one?" Charlie asked.

His sisters sniggered. Charlie pulled a face as he scrubbed the back of his neck. It had been a fair question and there was injustice in their determination to focus on the idea that he thought multiple of the Pence brothers cute, and not consider that he was at a loss as to which brother his lesbian sisters might bestow such an adjective upon.

"The little scruffy one," Susan answered.

Charlie considered the new information. It didn't answer the question.

He rinsed his hair in the basin, flinching at the cold water against his scalp, and then pulled the towel down from the side of the screen, roughly drying off. There was movement off to the side. Even patting his face dry, he could sense it.

"Don't—!" Charlie started, but it was futile. Clean clothes were deposited on the chest at the end of the screen as his dirty ones were stolen. As deeply as he objected to society's class structure on principle, there was a strong argument to be made that Charlie considered himself an independent grown man, who didn't like people touching his things or being in his personal spaces, and who would have liked to be able to decry social injustices without Jasper shoving socks in his mouth to shut him up.

Alas, his sister had married into the nobility and dragged him kicking and screaming with her. Rebecca was intensely vocal in her opinion that Charlie couldn't look after himself, and unfortunately, every attempt to prove her wrong had failed in painfully dramatic fashion. He didn't have time to cause a scene, and quickly dressed himself in the new clothes. At least the coat had remained safe on the bed. He strode out to collect it, trying to ignore the stern eyes of his sisters.

"Where do you think you're going?" Rebecca demanded.

"To the morgue," Charlie replied, swinging himself into the long, ratty, tan coat. "I've made arrangements to consult with a junior doctor after the debacle last night."

"Have you just?" Susan commented warningly.

Charlie flicked out his collar, dismissing the warning in her tone.

"Of all the medical professionals I have dealt with recently, she seems by far the most agreeable, and I am interested in her opinion," Charlie replied. "Something must be done. Women are *dying*. Families are grieving. Ladies from the High Houses are too frightened to leave their buildings—"

"It's not just ladies from the High Houses," Rebecca interrupted nervously.

Charlie eyed her tone and posture. His eyes narrowed.

"You don't need to worry, Becky," he assured.

"I'm worrying for her," Susan countered. "And what makes you so sure?"

Charlie considered the question. "Neither of you fit the pattern of traits the current victims share. You're above the age bracket, albeit only slightly, and the physical characteristics are all wrong."

"Really?" Susan arched an eyebrow.

"Yes," Charlie answered like he wasn't sure why she was doubting him. "I know Becky used to work for Bronny, but so did a great many people, and it is only current escorts being targeted."

"So there is a pattern?" Rebecca sighed. "You're already burrowing down the rabbit hole, aren't you, Charlie?"

"Have been for a while…" he mused, brow creased in thought. "Long enough to know I'm doing something wrong this time. There's a piece I'm missing… something crucial." His lips pursed into a small thin frown as he thought. "That's where Florin comes in…" he finished, patting his pockets absentmindedly and heading for the door.

"Florin?" Susan called after him. "Amelia Florin? Lord Pound's little girl? Has she graduated already?"

"Graduates tomorrow," Charlie called back, heading for the stairs. "Fortunately, her education was accumulative and doesn't require physical possession of her degree to be useful." He heard both of them roll their eyes that time. There was such an intense judgement in their silence. He carefully dodged the silverware trolley on his way out and shut the door on their opinions.

# 3

The day was turning into beautiful sunshine and Amy was loathe to leave it behind for the cold white tiles and sterile light of the morgue. Still, at least she wasn't going alone. Her original plan for the morning had been to join her friends to pick up their graduation gowns and go for tea. Tea had been cancelled as she attempted to make her apologies because Laura and Jane asked if they could help. They probably could. Amy certainly wasn't going to turn them down. She knew exactly how they felt. They all wanted to save lives.

She led the way down the corridor towards the back of the hospital. Laura and Jane trailed her arm-in-arm. Her friends' curiosities had been piqued, but it wasn't just about the case.

"Do you remember that piece in the tabloids a few years ago, when Shilling had just started to make a name for himself?" Laura asked cheekily. "They said he was an escaped lunatic that Lord Pound had pardoned in return for his innate understanding of the criminal mind."

Amy gave an exasperated sigh and Jane chuckled at both of them.

"None of that is true," Amy grumbled. "Shilling isn't

a criminal, he isn't insane, and he's never been committed. Daddy wouldn't let him work like he does if that were the case."

"Don't let Harry hear you talking like that," Jane warned, as they pushed through the double doors blocking the wide corridor. They strode into the last section of corridor, heading for the door on their right that would take them into the morgue at the back. Someone was loitering there already, and it wasn't the someone Amy had been expecting. She started when she saw him. Harry raised an eyebrow at her and pulled himself off the wall. His chocolate brown coat was neatly fitted and matched his perfectly combed hair. He would have been painfully handsome, if he wasn't stained with judgement.

"Don't let Harry hear you talking like what?" he asked.

"Harry?" Amy exclaimed. "What are you doing here?"

"I could very well ask you the same question," he replied, striding over to join them. "Father told me you were coming here to meet Charles Shilling. Are you out of your mind? What are you doing associating with that lunatic?!"

"Told you," Jane grimaced softly.

"Shilling is trying to stop the Jack's murders," Amy defended. "We're going to help."

"We?" Harry turned his critical look on her friends.

"Hi Harry," Laura grinned at him, clutching Jane's arm and resting her head sweetly on her girlfriend's shoulder.

"Hi Laura," Harry replied, refusing to be undone by her winsomeness. He turned his attention back to Amy. "Amy, please, you can't be serious. The man is dangerous. For all we know, he is the killer!"

"You don't mean that," Amy insisted. "I know you don't like him, Harry, and I know he's uncomfortably eccentric, but he's not a killer. You know better than that. He's trying to help, and I can think of no worthier cause!"

Harry's face settled into stern disapproval. Amy took him by the shoulders and looked into his eyes.

"People are dying, Harry," she implored. "Girls our age, our peers, are being murdered! I didn't get into medicine just so that I could sit at home, wringing my hands, and lamenting tragedy. If the worst thing I do in all my years is associate with Charles Shilling in order to stop a killer, I don't think God will hold that against me."

Harry sighed, his shoulders slumping in surrender. He gently pulled Amy into his arms. She slipped her hands around his waist as he held her tightly and kissed the top of her head. He rested his cheek against her hair, and she swore she could feel him smile.

"You're right, of course," he muttered. "You're always right. I'm sorry, Amy. I don't mean to be a brute about it."

"I know." She hugged him back. "You're just being protective, Harry. I get it, but I'm not the one who needs protecting right now."

"Perhaps," Harry relented. "However, you'll forgive me for feeling otherwise? You're always going to be the one I feel needs protecting, I don't think I can help that."

She kissed his cheek. "That's sweet, provided you don't get possessive about it."

"Of course not," Harry grimaced. "I'm just trying to watch out for you, Amelia. You remember father was investigated after that blasted tabloid piece a few years ago? It was all Shilling's fault. He assaulted the paper's photographer."

"He didn't hurt anyone," Amy disagreed. "He just never consented to having his picture taken."

"He dumped a bucket of water over the man's camera!" Harry exclaimed.

"Ouch," Jane commented. "That's expensive equipment. No wonder they called him a madman."

"Exactly," Harry agreed. "He is. Man's a complete lunatic."

"Who's a complete lunatic?" Shilling asked from the doorway.

They all turned as one. Shilling had entered so softly none of them had heard him. Amy felt an uncomfortable guilt catch fire in her gut. He was regarding them so curiously, so earnestly.

"Who do you think?" Harry replied scathingly.

"Hm, of course," Shilling sighed, absentmindedly ruffling his blonde hair and completely missing the insult. "But we don't know for certain the Jack of Hearts is a man. The tabloids all refer to the killer as a man, but I have yet to see any solid evidence to support the theory." He smiled at Amy. "Thank you again, Miss Florin, for agreeing to help. I'm hoping a new perspective will shed some light on this gruesome case."

"Of course, Mister Shilling," she replied quickly, trying to hurry the conversation along. "These are my friends from school, Laura Mark and Jane Franc. I hope you don't mind, I told them what we were doing and they wanted to help. I thought given that the three of us are only junior doctors, perhaps more eyes would be better."

"Absolutely," Shilling nodded. "The more the merrier. Thank you for your assistance, ladies. Are you joining us as well, Pound Junior?"

"I think not…" Harry answered, giving the door to the morgue a look of deep apprehension.

"Are you sure?" Shilling checked. "It might be quite useful to have legal council in attendance, and there's nothing wrong with your eyes."

Harry looked like he was about to snarl in response when the morgue doors opened. They all turned as the mortician strode out and started in surprise, nearly colliding with the group. She looked over them all, wild-eyed for a moment, and then smiled.

"Harry Pound, what on earth are you doing all the way down here?" she asked.

"You have no idea how excellent a question that is, Monty," Harry sighed.

"And with these fine ladies and… this freak," Monty finished with an unimpressed glance at Shilling.

"We're not with the freak, I assure you," Harry promised.

Amy gave him a subtle but disapproving elbow. Monty's attention was still on Shilling.

"You're not allowed in my morgue, Mister Shilling," she informed him sternly. "I've told you before."

"I have permission from Lord Pound," Shilling countered. "I'm with Miss Florin and her associates. We're here to get a second opinion on last night's body."

"Ah," Monty turned back to Harry. "Now your presence is making an abrupt sort of sense..."

"I apologise, Monty," Harry grimaced. "I don't know what's gotten into my father and I haven't been able to talk the women out of it. For what it's worth, they are brilliant, well-meaning ladies. This is Miss Mark and Miss Franc, and, of course, Amelia..."

"Yes, the famous Amelia Florin," Monty held out her hand. "I know Harry from down at the Club, and he never stops talking about you."

Amy shook Monty's hand. Her fingers were freezing. The woman smiled knowingly at her. Amy didn't like it. She couldn't say exactly what was wrong, but there was something smug in the way Monty looked at her that set her on edge.

"I'm afraid he hasn't mentioned you to me," she replied as coolly as she dared. "However, you know Harry, he frequents quite a few clubs..."

She could feel Laura and Jane holding their breaths in the background, watching the tension rise. They would be loving this. The brink of scandal was a lot more exciting than tea and cake, so she felt no guilt at dragging them into it. Harry stayed unflinching at her comment, and Shilling seemed to watch the entire ordeal with mild fascination.

"Well, the son of the Lord Chief Justice is a popular man," Monty shrugged. "You're not the only woman who holds his heart, Miss Florin, Lady Luck seems to smile favourably at him as well."

Now Amy knew she didn't like the way Monty was looking at her. It felt like the mortician was leering at her, testing her to see if she was ruffled by Harry's pastimes. Amy was not one to crack under pressure, and she certainly wasn't going to discuss Harry's gambling in public. Before she could respond, Monty turned sharply towards Shilling. Shilling was ignoring everyone else and heading for the morgue door.

"Oi!" Monty snapped at him. "No! I've told you before, freak!"

"There is a loose killer and an aging corpse, we do not have time for pleasantries and introductions," Shilling insisted.

"Why haven't they locked you up for it yet?" Monty quipped.

"They did," Harry commented drily.

Amy glared at him. Harry caught the glare. He had the sense to look ashamed for a second, but then steadfastly ignored her reproval.

"They locked him up and then let him back out?" Monty raised an eyebrow. "Why release the freak of nature? I can't think of a more likely suspect, given what he does to the bodies."

"They're dead, Monty," Shilling sighed. "They can't feel anything, and I need to know what these women are being stabbed with. Sticking a few knives in some cadavers should not be a crime."

"It's a butcher's knife, Shilling," Monty glowered. "I've already told you."

"It isn't a butcher's knife," Shilling muttered. "Look, I won't touch anything. The ladies can look for me, but I want another opinion. The papers keep talking about a dagger, but the incision is clearly being made with a knife — it only has a blade on one side, and the blade is serrated — so it's not a butcher's knife."

Silence reigned in the wake of his declaration. Amy watched him curiously. Shilling fidgeted with the buttons on the front of his coat and stared at the floor. He didn't seem to like all the eyes on him, but he didn't know what else to do to move his investigation forward without drawing attention. Harry sighed at him.

"Why didn't they just leave you in prison and see if the killings stopped?" he quipped.

Amy glared at her fiancé, but this time he knew to ignore her completely. She wasn't going to let him get away with it. Disliking Shilling was no excuse for his behaviour.

"Because Mister Shilling hasn't killed anyone," she declared, feeling a desperate need for someone to defend the uncomfortable investigator. She reached into her pocket to produce the letter her father had given her. "This is from Lord Pound," she announced, holding the letter out to Monty. "It asks your boss very nicely to let myself and my associates, including Mister Shilling, have a look at the body that was found last night."

"Nepotism in action," Monty bowed invitingly, extending an arm towards the morgue door. "How could I refuse?"

She didn't even look at the letter. Amy kept it clasped in her fingers, unsure what else to do with it, as she stood tall and moved towards the door.

"Amy," Harry tried one last desperate attempt to keep her back. "You really don't have to do this."

She turned to him, making sure he caught the full brunt of the glare he'd been trying to avoid.

"Go back to work, Harry," she instructed. "I'll see you this evening."

Now he had the sense to look sorry. She could see the apology in his eyes, but it didn't make it to his lips. He wasn't sorry for what he'd said, he was just sorry it had upset her. He moved to kiss her and she shied from it. His lips brushed her cheek.

"Ouch," Monty smirked, eyeing the cold-shoulder. "Careful not to speak your mind, Harry. Sounds like she doesn't approve."

"And you," Amy turned on the mortician. "Are you an active saboteur or are you just grossly incompetent? I've met you for all of two minutes and I can see exactly why Mister Shilling is asking for help if this is the way you and your bosses treat him." She looked between Monty and Harry. "What are either of you doing to stop these killings? At least Mister Shilling is trying, and all I've seen you two do is bully him for his efforts. I don't know how you can treat this matter with anything less than the gravity it deserves, but I expect better."

Monty looked little more than entertained by the attack, but Harry looked ashamed.

"Sorry Amy…" he muttered bashfully. "You-you're

right. I'm sorry."

"Good," she stated. "Shape up or ship out, Harry. I've got work to do."

He nodded. "I-I'll see you later..." He thrust his hands in his pockets and turned away, striding from the room.

Monty gave a low whistle as she watched him go. Amy glared at her, but the mortician just shrugged.

"Really thought he might try and swoop in and save the day like something out of Euripides after that speech," she commented. "Secret doctor Harry Pound to the rescue."

"I think not," Amy glowered at the woman, heading for the morgue again and leading the way through the door.

"Yes, unfortunately, Harry's rather squeamish," Jane admitted as they all followed Amy into the cold, pale back room.

"What? That Harry?" Monty scoffed.

"I would also like to offer my doubts on the assertion," Shilling chipped in.

"Don't agree with me, freak," Monty warned.

"No, he is," Laura insisted. "We've tried talking shop with Amy a few times while Harry's around, and he always goes all pale and leaves the room. Can't even stand surgical stories, let alone having to see actual blood."

They all stopped silently, beholding Jenny's bloodstained corpse on the slab. Amy stared. Jenny had dark red curls like her, but they were matted with blood. It was so easy to see herself in all the dead women. A sharp chill sank through her bones, but it was too bleak to cause a shudder. The dead were not her specialty. Everything she had learnt had been in the name of saving lives — but so was this.

Jane and Laura were still holding hands as the three of them slowly approached the body. Amy knew she had to take the lead, but part of her wished she didn't. Jenny was staring at the ceiling with unblinking, clouded eyes. Her skin was grey with death, and a giant, dark, bloody cavity marred her bare chest. Dried blood still coated her torso and throat, where another dark wound stained her skin.

"Poor thing…" Laura commented softly.

Jane and Amy both nodded and made small sounds of agreement.

"All right, ladies," Amy sighed. "Gown up."

The three of them donned aprons and gloves over their dresses before they got to work. Shilling perched himself on an empty slab nearby, close enough to see, but well out of Monty's way. Monty went back to her desk in the corner of the room, where she put her feet up and began eating a sandwich. Amy didn't comment, but she did raise an eyebrow. She couldn't believe Harry could be on a first name basis with someone like Monty, and yet disapprove of Shilling over a few quirks.

"I still can't believe Harry Pound is squeamish," Monty commented, as though to herself.

"Harry's a gentleman," Laura remarked. "He has a gentleman's disposition."

"Whatever that means," Monty grinned at them.

"It means he's handsome, charming, and rich," Jane clarified with a chuckle.

"Harry's a soft soul, really," Amy defended, as she began to inspect the wounds on Jenny's body. "He plays at being dignified, but he's quite delicate and easily flustered."

"He has the most delicate sensibilities of anyone I've met," Jane chuckled. "You remember how embarrassed he got when you were talking to us after the second year exams?"

"Oh! The sex talk," Laura giggled. "Oh yes, he was having none of that!"

"He's just a bit prudish," Amy commented, slightly glad that their silly gossip distracted from the gruesomeness of the task at hand. "Harry's a private person."

"Now I know you're having me on," Monty scoffed.

"Not at all," Amy disagreed.

"She's telling the truth," Jane affirmed. "I don't know if he gets a bit laddish down at the clubs, but Harry's very sex shy."

"He and Amy are waiting 'til marriage," Laura teased.

"Laura!" Amy scolded.

Laura smiled winsomely at her, and Amy melted slightly. Laura had large dark eyes like a doe, and the cutest, sweetest smile. She was a dreadful gossip, but she meant well and her heart was always in the right place. It was very hard to stay cross with her. Still, Amy gave her 'the look'. She didn't need her private affairs aired here.

"Which is crazy…" Jane added slyly, scrolling her measuring tape against the wounds and noting down her findings. "You'd think living under the same roof would give you the perfect opportunity to get some experimenting done."

"Well, maybe for you it would," Amy preened. "Harry and I are different. We're very privileged to be betrothed, so we haven't had to worry about finding someone. It let us focus on our studies and, now, finally, we'll be able to set a date after graduation. I'm looking forward to it."

"So are we," Laura beamed. "I love weddings."

"She does love weddings, but she's mostly invested in you getting Harry's pants off," Jane teased them.

"Nosy," Amy berated. Her friends grinned at her. She shifted around the slab and caught Shilling watching them. There was a pained tension around his grey eyes as they measured the damage on the girl's body. Amy couldn't place it, but it reminded her of her own grief for Jenny's tragic demise. It brought the reality back, and she struggled to maintain her distraction.

"You're being awfully quiet, freak," Monty called to him.

"I have nothing to add," Shilling answered softly, fidgeting with the signet ring on his middle finger. "No one is discussing the case. Everyone's just lying and laughing about it and I don't know why. It's none of my business."

"Nobody's lying," Amy replied in confusion.

"You lied just before," Shilling motioned to her.

"Moments ago, you lied about looking forward to your wedding."

"That wasn't a lie," Amy snapped. She could see in his eyes he didn't believe her, and a hot irritation fluttered in her chest. "It wasn't!" she insisted. "I am looking forward to my wedding. You know, Mister Shilling, unfounded comments like that are why Harry doesn't like you. It is deeply rude to spout theories like that, even if you don't realise it."

Shilling wouldn't meet her eye. His serious grey gaze was inspecting the ceiling and one awkward hand rubbed his crooked mouth like he wished he could wipe the words away.

"Apologies, I must have been mistaken," he muttered half-heartedly. No one believed him. He certainly didn't believe himself. He went back to twisting his ring.

Amy glared, scrolling her memories of the previous conversation. They'd just been gossiping. No one had told any lies. Yet, her friends were watching her warily now. They knew she was irritated. Well, it wasn't like her poker face was practiced. It was the first time she had come under Shilling's direct observation, and she almost felt bad for snapping at Harry earlier. She hadn't realised just how annoying the sleuth could be.

"Let's just keep to the work," Amy muttered.

Laura and Jane nodded at her, their eyes supportive and their carefree gossip loyally sealed away for later. The flashes of shared looks between them were adamant this would be discussed at length later, but not in front of Shilling.

"Death seems to have been caused by this single wound to the neck," Jane commented, bringing them on track.

"Stabbed in the throat to bleed out, and then heart removed after," Amy agreed. "Definitely a knife, not a dagger."

"Report!" Monty called out with her mouth full, holding up a file.

Laura went over and took it from her. She flicked it open as she came back and leafed through the pages.

"That lines up," she agreed with the findings comparing them to the notes Jane and Amy had already taken.

"Oh look, I can measure..." Monty drawled sarcastically around her sandwich.

"This says a butcher's knife made these wounds, and that the girl was sexually assaulted," Laura commented dubiously.

"Yeah," Monty affirmed.

"I see no evidence for that," Amy disagreed.

"This wasn't a butcher's knife," Jane agreed. "I can see why someone would speculate that, given the size, but the blade is at least partially serrated — see here."

"And there are no defensive wounds," Amy added. "She never fought back. Someone surprised her."

"This wasn't a frenzied attack, it was straight out murder," Laura agreed. "There are signs of sexual activity, but nothing to suggest an assault. She was working as an escort, coming back from a job. There's nothing here to suggest the person she had sex with is the one who killed her."

"Oh, come on," Monty grumbled. "That is far and away the most likely scenario."

"Not in this case it isn't," Amy disagreed. "Let me see the wound again, Jane." Amy sidled up beside her friend, trying to focus on the work now that there was no other distraction, and ignore the fact that they were prying over the body of someone who had been very alive this time yesterday. She inspected the wound in Jenny's throat carefully, peering through Jane's magnifying glass. "The angle of this wound makes it look like she was grabbed from behind and stabbed in the front…"

"A surprise attack," Laura nodded. "Hence no time to defend herself."

"That lines up with the spray patterns from the scenes," Shilling offered. "The Jack seems to strike each woman in the throat, severing their oesophagus and artery, which stops them from screaming and causes them to bleed out quickly, but in order for the blood to spray uninterrupted, which it appears to do, they would need to be positioned behind their victims."

"These are messy deaths," Jane said. "Interesting that the Jack chooses such a filthy means of murder, yet does their best to keep themselves clean."

"If they were doing this to bathe in the blood of their victims, someone would have caught them a long time ago," Amy sighed. "Unless they had a private killing space, but the killings have all been in public places."

"Even in London you can't exactly walk around covered in blood without attracting attention," Laura agreed. "And why cut out the hearts? What does that even achieve?"

"They're trophies," Shilling shrugged like it was obvious. "The killer takes the hearts of these women as trophies. That part is simple."

"Oh really?" Monty drawled at him. "That part is simple, is it? You little psycho."

Shilling gave the mortician a confused look, and Amy felt her irritation at him soften slightly. He really didn't get it. He could see how things worked, and he had no idea why other people couldn't. It was obvious to him. She felt like she understood too, and she had some sympathy for his struggle.

"Stealing someone's heart is symbolic of desire or love," Amy stated. "But are we looking for someone who wanted these women to love them or who considered their love stolen by them?"

"Two very possible theories," Shilling nodded at her encouragingly. "Not the only two theories, but good theories nonetheless. I feel as though the tabloids have been pushing in favour of the former — some Jack who's more than a little touched in the head kills beautiful escorts and steals their hearts forever, out of some deranged fantasy of love."

"That's definitely the story the papers are telling," Laura agreed. "But they also depict the Jack with a dagger, and this was absolutely not a dagger."

"It looks like it could be a hunting knife…" Amy mused.

Everyone looked at her. She was peering at the injury in Jenny's neck and didn't notice their eyes on her at first, but found the room watching her when she looked up to investigate the silence.

"You know, the partially serrated blade? Designed to cut through hide." she pressed. "A hunting knife makes the most sense. I've seen the ones Daddy and Harry use when they go deer hunting, and either of them would work well to stab someone quickly and then cut out their heart like this. There's nothing surgical about these incisions, but it seems a bit more meticulous than simply butchering. I wouldn't be surprised if we were looking for a hunter."

Shilling slipped off his slab and approached the ladies around Jenny. He stepped up at Amy's side and peered curiously over her shoulder.

"That's excellent work, Miss Florin," he praised. "Truly brilliant." He stepped back and stroked his chin. "And a brand new theory to go with my other one."

"Your other one?" Amy asked.

"Initially I was pondering if, rather than the nonsense the tabloids were pushing, much like the latter consideration of your earlier question, there was perhaps a woman killing these ladies out of jealousy," Shilling wondered. "I am loathe to consider that motive under usual circumstances, but the conditions of this case have me flummoxed. I followed all the usual suspects of predatory men stalking these women and came up with dead ends. It is possible that a woman who considers these ladies thieves of her love could be the Jack of Hearts."

"She'd have to be a tall, strong lady to be able to grab them from behind, stab them in the throat, and hold them face down to bleed out," Monty pointed out scathingly.

"She would," Jane agreed. "But both you and I could fit that bill. It's certainly not impossible, especially if she hunts."

"You or I had the height and strength to maybe kill this poor girl," Monty corrected. "Some of the other ladies that have lain on that slab... not so much. The fifth one... what's her name...?"

"Theresa," Shilling answered. "She was the tallest. Still not outside the realms of possibility for you, Monty. You've got a mean left hook, and I'm wagering the Jack gets by a lot on the element of surprise. Whoever they are, they're not someone anyone suspects. These killings have been going on for a year, becoming more frequent, and still these women are surprised by the person who attacks them."

"It's not me," Monty growled at him.

"Nor me," Shilling replied. "But I had my suspicions regarding the autopsies, and I'm pleased I had some other eyes consider the evidence. I know it's easy to get caught up in a good story, but there is no hard evidence to suggest that the women are being killed by a male lover. I need to broaden my search." He looked to Amy and her friends and gave them a grateful nod. "Thank you, ladies. I appreciate your willingness to share your expertise."

"You're welcome," Laura smiled at him.

"It's not exactly expertise, Shilling," Jane replied, as they all began to remove their gloves and aprons. "We're not coroners, although I'll credit Amy's genius theory of the hunting knife."

"So would I," Shilling smiled. "And perhaps the coroners will take their jobs more seriously now that they've been shown up by a group of junior doctors."

Monty made an obscene gesture in his direction. Shilling ignored it. As far as Amy could tell the mortician was getting sloppy in her effort to keep Shilling away from her and her work. It sounded like she might not have been the only one. That didn't bode well for the profession, but perhaps if Shilling could annoy them into sloppy work, he could also use Amy and her friends to annoy them back into competency. That, or something far more nefarious was afoot.

"What will you do now?" she asked him.

"Follow the case, Miss Florin," he answered.

She nodded slowly, but her mind was spinning quickly. They packed away their things, farewelled Monty and her compulsive rudeness, and left the building. She wasn't sorry to be out of the morgue. The sunshine was pleasant and it eased the weight sitting like coal over her heart. Jane and Laura were arm-in-arm again, and their eyes were already prepared to start gossiping the minute Shilling was out of sight. Shilling, in turn, gave them a polite nod and turned to walk up the street. The black weight clenched.

"Mister Shilling!" Amy hailed him, surprising even herself.

He turned back to them, absentmindedly patting his pockets and raising his eyebrows curiously.

"I…" she stuttered weakly, half her brain trying to work out what the hell she was doing. "I… don't suppose you want any help following the case…?"

Shilling cocked his head to the side curiously, that way he did. Good God, it really did look like a puppy. It was a puppy look.

"If you want to help, Miss Florin, I'm not opposed…" he offered. There was a hesitation in his voice that made Amy wonder if that was a lie, except it didn't seem like one. Shilling didn't lie. That wasn't his style. It was more likely that he didn't understand why she was offering and was hedging his bets in case he had misread the situation. Given the way she'd snapped at him earlier it wasn't wholly unfair. His eyebrows shot up earnestly again. "You might prefer to offer your services to Scotland Yard, if you're looking to bring the Jack to justice."

"Yes," Amy agreed. "Perhaps. Yet… yet, if I actually wanted to bring the Jack of Hearts to justice, my efforts would almost certainly be better spent serving your case, would they not?"

"They would," Shilling nodded, unable to engage in the polite white lies of modesty.

Amy smiled despite herself. She looked back at Jane and Laura. Laura was grinning at her in open support, but Jane raised a concerned eyebrow like she was worried Amy was going mad.

"I'm going to go help him," she announced.

"Do you want us to come too?" Jane asked.

"Do you want to come too?" Amy replied.

"Not really…" Laura admitted. "I've had enough murder for one day, and I want some time to prepare before graduation tomorrow, but you'll tell us what you find?"

"And you'll send someone if you need us?" Jane added.

"Of course," Amy nodded.

Laura gave a nervous squeak and hugged Amy tightly, kissing her cheek.

"Be safe! Make good life choices!" she instructed.

"I think I am," Amy smiled. The lump of coal in her chest had vanished. That certainly felt like a good life choice. She farewelled her friends and then turned to Shilling, who was waiting patiently and curiously like a well-trained Labrador. Scratch that, a well-trained scruffy mutt of unintelligible blonde pedigree, but unusual cunning and intellect. She made a mental note to never repeat that comparison to his face. He gave her a nod as she joined him, and they headed off up the street.

"Where to first?" she asked.

"Madam Bronny's High House," he answered. "That's the last place anyone reliable will have seen Jenny Kent alive."

"The station's that way—" she began, noting his direction.

"No," Charlie cut her off. "No Underground. Absolutely not."

"It's perfectly safe—" she began again, but cut herself off. There was a set in his eye and his mouth that caused her to fall silent. That must be one idiosyncrasy off the extensive list of quirks she had heard Mister Shilling had. It looked like they were walking. That was fine too.

# 4

Bronny's High House was a sprawling Mayfair mansion with a particularly wealthy clientele. The façade was polished marble and every room was designed to invoke atmosphere. Shilling led the way up the front steps like he owned the place, and Florin followed him quickly, trying to mask her apprehension.

The entrance hall was grand. Its floor was a polished design of brass and black marble, with matching pillars that disappeared into a ceiling of chandeliers. Couches and divans were spaced between draping sheer curtains that allowed people to wait comfortably in an imitation of privacy, but a gap was left like a corridor down the centre to a stained mahogany counter at the back. Sweeping staircases ascended from either side of the counter into the depths of the building.

A girl in a short frilled skirt, elaborate corsetry, and not much else, was sitting behind the counter. She squealed delightedly when she saw them striding towards her and bounced out from behind the desk.

"Charlie!" she cried, throwing her arms around his neck and kissing his cheek.

"Hello Lizzie," Shilling kissed her cheek politely in return.

"It's true, isn't it?" Lizzie gripped him by the sleeves, her voice catching. "In the paper… about Jenny…"

"It is," Shilling admitted.

Lizzie turned her face away, her eyes filling with tears, and pressed a hand to her trembling lips.

"I told her…" she whispered, her voice shaking. "I told her not to go…"

"What happened?" Shilling asked. "Please, Lizzie, as much detail as you can."

"Jenny got a job last night," Lizzie shrugged tearfully. "It was a call out and I told her not to go. She-she said it would be fine. She said because of what happened to the girl from Dawes House this week we should all be safe for now…" Lizzie pressed her fingers to her tears as they started to spill. Her voice shook as sobs broke her report. "I don't know where she went! *Hic*–! She-she just said it was e-e-easy work, and the m-money was too good to-to t-turn down. *Hic*–! She said it wasn't far… but she didn't s-s-say w-where! *Hic*–!"

Shilling rubbed her shoulder soothingly. Lizzie pulled a handkerchief from the front of her corset and dabbed at her tears. Amy watched the whole ordeal unfold, feeling strangely numb. Shilling jerked his head towards the desk. Lizzie nodded, wiping her streaming face. She led them both around the back of the counter and through the door behind it.

On the other side of the door was a room so full of noise and people Amy was surprised they hadn't heard it from the entrance hall. It was arranged in a similar fashion to the other room, with extensive cushioned seating arrangements and flowing curtains. There was an obvious kitchenette up the back beside a sleek dark staircase. The people in the room ranged more than she'd ever seen, in both attire and age.

Clusters of people in skimpy outfits clearly looked like workers, but they mingled casually with others in perfectly ordinary clothes who could have been visitors, clients, relatives, or workers themselves. One of the curtained areas contained a cluster of well-dressed children playing together.

Shilling called out to someone, signalling the tearful Lizzie. Another worker rolled their eyes and excused themselves from their conversation to go and front the desk. Amy felt herself getting eyeballed by them as they strode by. She had never been in a High House before and had no idea if it showed. She hadn't known what to expect, and didn't know if this was it. A few people were catching sight of them now, and Amy was surprised by the warmness of their reception. Well, not hers, but several people called out 'Charlie' with all the enthusiasm Lizzie had shown. He patted the girl's shoulder again and slipped through the crowd.

Amy squirmed uncomfortably. She had no idea where to go or what to do, except to watch where he went. It didn't feel right to follow him into the crowd, not when he'd just abandoned her and Lizzie near the door.

"He's very popular here then?" she asked nervously.

"Charlie?" Lizzie queried. "Of course. Everyone loves him."

"Pays well, does he?" Amy replied.

"Pays?" Lizzie gave her a look. "Charlie doesn't

shop here. He's family."

"Family…?" Amy echoed, but her quiet confusion was lost in the din. She watched as Shilling spoke quickly to a few people, slipping through the crowd. A toy ball rolled out of the children's play area. Shilling stopped it with his foot, almost absentmindedly, mid-conversation. He turned as a little girl ran out to collect it. She slowed as she approached him. He picked up the ball, holding it under his arm as he signed at her. The girl signed back. Shilling smiled, crouching down to meet her eye as he and the child held a conversation with their hands. The girl grinned at him. He gave her back the ball and ruffled her curls. She poked him playfully in the arm before running off.

"He grew up here," Lizzie offered, seemingly sensing Amy's confusion. "Well, for a little while. After their father died, his sister Becky came to work here. She brought Charlie with her. He was a bit too nosy for his own good, even back then, but he's always been very loyal. This is where Becky met her wife, although they were seeing each other for over a year before Susan proposed."

"Huh," was all Amy managed in reply.

"Charlie!" a sharp yell cut over the chatter. Everyone turned to the voice. One of the curtains was pulled aside to reveal an open doorway. A mature woman in a tightly laced red dress stood there, her curls piled fashionably atop her head. When she called, the whole room fell silent. She was staring through the crowd at Shilling with a look that could kill. With a deliberate slowness, she raised a hand and curled a finger at him.

Shilling gave her a nod. He looked to Amy and jerked his head at the woman in the doorway, inviting her to follow. She did. It wasn't like she had anywhere else to be. They met partway across the room and began approaching the door together. Conversation was starting to resume, but people were watching them go.

The woman Amy could only presume was Madam Bronny had disappeared back into her room, but left the door ajar for them. Amy let Shilling take the lead. He was the one who had been summoned, after all. It was a well-known rule of the city that no one messed with the Madams of the High Houses. They were just as likely to go after those that wronged them illegally as legally, and their methods could be ruthless. Officially, they would never condone such actions. Unofficially, there was a rumour that they had pooled their resources to offer a bounty to anyone who could bring them the dripping, bloody heart of the Jack killing their girls.

Shilling slowed as they neared the door. His head turned and his eyes narrowed at something in a different direction.

"Swift...?" he murmured so softly Amy wasn't sure if she heard him properly.

She followed his gaze. He was looking at a man in the crowd, one of the few who wasn't looking at them. Tall, dark, and handsome, half dressed in nothing more than black trousers and a waistcoat. His dark curls hung nearly to his shoulders. The man didn't see them, but Shilling was definitely looking. He looked away just as quickly and strode through the doorway. Amy followed close behind.

Inside was an office more lavish than any she'd seen before, and she lived in a Lord's manor. The giant polished desk was long enough to lie across, heavily stacked bookcases lined the walls, pedestals with adornments Amy could only assume were art or sex toys or both had been placed around the room, and shaded lamps gave the space a seductive atmosphere. The woman in the red dress was lounging in a chair behind the desk. She eyed them as they entered. Shilling shut the door behind them. Amy could feel a nervous sweat prickling her back.

"Tell me you're not screwing me around, Charlie," Bronny demanded. She gave Amy a dismissive glance. "I'm not hiring bait."

"Bronny, this is Doctor Florin. Florin, this is Madam Bronny," Shilling made official introductions with respectful deference. "Florin is helping with the case, Bron. Needed another set of eyes in the morgue. I'm sorry about Jenny…"

"Not as sorry as I am," she muttered. She gave Amy another eyeballing, this time with more consideration. "You're Pound's girl?"

"Yes, Madam," Amy curtsied gently.

"Congratulations on your qualification," Bronny purred. "I had heard you were something of an exotic beauty. Pity you picked medicine as your calling. You could have made a fortune here."

Amy blushed.

"She's marrying Harry Pound, she doesn't need another fortune," Shilling dismissed, perching himself on the edge of Bronny's desk and twisting his ring.

Bronny gave his choice in seat a direct look, but he ignored it. "Tell me about Jenny," he requested.

Bronny took a moment, but since Shilling didn't care that he was sitting on the edge of her desk, she chose not to either.

"She left last night without my permission," Bronny sighed. "One of the other girls covered for her. Stupid tits, both of them. I can't believe they would be so reckless! Apparently, Jenny got offered a job worth enough to make her careless. No one's been able to give me an exact number yet."

"You think that's deliberate?" Shilling asked.

Bronny reached into a drawer in her desk. She pulled out a slim folder and smacked it down on the polished surface.

"I have been talking with the other Madams who've lost women to the Jack," she announced. "We're finally managing to get some truth out of the investigators, our idiots, and civilians. Every single girl we've lost has been offered a job so well-paid they couldn't turn it down and then been murdered and robbed. They all have their purses missing and they've never been recovered."

"That's not unusual," Amy replied. "There are plenty of people in the city who would rob a body before reporting it, and the dead women have been found in poorer areas."

"Which was something I had thought before as well," Shilling agreed. "However, I have since received more intel on the matter. Word on the street came back last week that the first people on the scene aren't finding anything to take — which implies the Jack is the thief as well as the killer."

"Do you think it could be about money?" Amy mused. "Robbing wealthy escorts sounds like an effective get-rich-quick scheme. The mutilation could be a cover up to disguise the motivation?"

"I like the way you think," Shilling smiled at her. "I wouldn't rule the theory out, but I feel that such mutilation is a steep risk to take over some coins."

"Also," Amy pulled a face, "the more I think about the idea… I just… cutting out someone's heart? Maybe it's just me, but that feels like such an intimate mutilation to cover a robbery."

"Not everyone has your empathy, child," Bronny sighed. "But I agree, something darker is afoot." She tapped a finger on her file. "There was something else we found, Charlie. I know you don't think any of the men booking these women are the killer… but you've never found the direct bookings that led to their deaths."

"I can't imagine why they wouldn't want to be found…" Shilling drawled.

"Stop dodging me, boy," she warned. "I know you seem to think you've ruled out men preying on these women, but we've all compared notes. To the best of our knowledge, every single one of them went to work at an inn the night they were killed. Not the same one, mind you, but every single lady was called out, and none of them were house calls. All of them were taken to booked rooms to work. The innkeepers we've managed to talk to all admit to seeing a tall man with a dark moustache, and a booking name of 'Denarius'."

"Denarius is as common a name as Smith," Amy commented. "I've heard some people use it as a cover name, due to its prevalence. And tall man with a dark moustache probably describes a quarter of London."

"Roughly a fifth of people using the name 'Denarius' to buy sex are using it as a cover," Shilling agreed. "Interesting about the inns though. I hadn't found that. Everyone I spoke to said they had been called out to jobs, but no one knew exactly where. I thought some of them were house calls."

"Maybe, some we still can't trace," Bronny admitted. "But people are being more open about it now, and what we have been able to find leads to booked rooms."

"By more open you mean their colleagues are starting to suddenly remember details? Or are finally prepared to admit details they previously omitted to protect themselves? Or they heard someone's story about an inn and a man with a moustache and now everyone wants a piece of it?" Shilling asked.

Bronny glared at him. Shilling met her look. Amy was surprised how nonplussed he was. Perhaps she shouldn't have been, given the way he was with everyone, but the Madam intimidated her, and Amy was a little bit impressed that Charlie could outstare someone so severe. He slipped off the desk and strode closer to her, holding her eye the entire way.

"I know you're angry," he sighed. "I know you're frightened and desperate, you have every right to be, but I have to do this my way, Bronny. You can conduct an investigation your way, no one's stopping you, but I have to follow the way I think and the evidence I have. Seven months! I've been working this God-awful case for seven months! It's the longest I've spent on anything! I have interviewed 257 people. I have had 43 degenerates arrested for their behaviour, but no one cares about them because they're not the Jack. I don't know what I'm missing. You know that horrible feeling where you know you don't know something, but you don't know what it is because you don't know it? I'm starting to feel like I'm drowning in it. I've been searching for the man killing these women for months and come up empty handed — that means I'm looking in the wrong direction."

"That's why you want to start focusing on female suspects?" Amy asked.

"Exactly," Shilling broke eye contact with Bronny and pointed at Amy. "Are there any women in the industry who might be taking out the competition? Were any of these ladies taking on dangerous jobs? Were they selling out to supposedly monogamist clients with jealous wives?"

"I can't hand out client information, Charlie," Bronny grimaced. "You know that. Not even for this. People have a right to privacy."

"They do," Shilling shrugged. "But if I were you, I would compare names with the other Madams. If anything suspicious crops up, I'd let me know."

"I will," Bronny nodded. "But I can tell you that nothing obvious has popped up so far, beyond what you've already caught." She paused a moment, as though sucking on a sour cherry. "You really think one of our own girls could be doing this?"

"He's not ruling out any theories," Amy answered.

"I am not," Shilling agreed. "If there is a tall man with a moustache out there who needs investigating, I will find them. Still, off the top of my head, I can think of a dozen people the investigation has run into who fit that bill, and I have ruled them all out as suspects already."

"We'll find who did this, Madam," Amy assured. "I promise."

"We?" Bronny echoed. "Charlie, tell me you're not letting this girl get involved?"

"I'm already involved," Amy retorted. "I wouldn't have thought you'd be the type to disapprove of my involvement. Madam, I have sat idly by while the body count has climbed over the last year, and it has been horrifying. I swear, I can see myself in every girl that shows up dead in the paper, and I couldn't bear it if I had to see another one. You must know how that feels. I'm sure that Shilling is brilliant, as people like you and my father so often tout, but he clearly needs help, and I have expertise he doesn't. I will not sit this out anymore."

Bronny raised an eyebrow at Shilling, who was poking around her shelves.

"She's marrying Harry Pound, is she?" Bronny disapproved, her expression speaking volumes on the perceived waste.

"So she says," Shilling replied, digging into an engraved tin and stealing a boiled sweet. "He's not smart enough for her." He looked up and held the tin out to Amy, offering her a sweet like he hadn't just insulted her fiancé.

She tried to stare him down, to make him realise what he had just said, but it was pointless. Shilling just watched her with those curious grey eyes, oblivious to the concept that what he had said was anything other than plain truth. Finally, she relented and shook her head at the candy. He shrugged and set it back on the shelf, sucking on his sweet.

"She might be too smart for you, Charlie," Bronny grinned at him.

"Unlikely," Shilling replied. "But I do like her brain."

Bronny smiled fondly as she watched him pace her office. "You could have been so expensive if I'd ever been able to convince you to like more about people than their brains..."

Shilling crinkled his nose in distaste. Even Amy couldn't help but smile at the expression. She'd been a little confused by the statement, given that she knew plenty of men more handsome than Shilling — but he could be accidentally cute when he forgot about being obnoxious, and surely the Madam would know how to market him to the right crowd.

"Why don't you want me involving Florin?" he shifted the subject back.

"Good God, Charlie, look at her!" Bronny exclaimed, gesturing. She looked back at Amy and met her eye with a mix of exasperation and concern. "I'm not trying to be an alarmist, sweetheart, but you're not the only one who sees yourself in those girls. If I put every girl we've lost to the Jack in a barrel and rolled them down to the river, the mix I'd tip out at the end would look like you. I didn't make that bait comment when you arrived to be snide — but insomuch as we could even figure the Jack has a type, I would say it would be you. If you're getting involved in this, you need to be careful."

Amy stood frozen at the warning. It was one thing to feel her own fear and grief for the dead women, it was something else entirely to hear another person air their trepidations. She had thought her concern limited to one human being caring about her fellow people. Madam Bronny made her sound like an active target.

"You have a point there," Shilling agreed slowly. "I should have seen that earlier. I kept seeing the girls as singular pieces rather than a whole... but when you do look at them as a whole it does look like our lady Florin here, doesn't it? Hm..." he glanced at Amy. "You're lucky you went into medicine instead of a House, Doctor Florin. You might have been the perfect target."

She knew he didn't mean it as a threat, but her blood chilled anyway. It was the offhand way he stated things that made them seem like the only possible truth. What he meant was the women had all had either dark skin or auburn hair, but it was just as easy to say everyone who had been killed had curls — which suggested half of London was in danger. Besides, it wasn't enough that they were all young women with curly hair — they were also all escorts, which meant Amy wasn't really a target.

Yet, his comment still rattled down in the bottom of

her stomach. It was a good thing she had never gone into a House. There was no way he knew. Even Shilling, who everyone claimed had that annoying habit of knowing things about you no one should know, he wouldn't know about that.

"We're not trying to scare you, child," Bronny assured. "Not more than any reasonable person would already be scared. We might all think little Charlie here is brilliant for what he does, but he is a magnet for chaos, and I've never seen him drag someone else into his anarchy — especially the daughter-in-law of Lord Pound. I just want you to be careful. I want at least one of you to be careful, and God knows it won't be Charlie."

Shilling stuck his sweet to the side of his mouth to stick his tongue out at the Madam. She didn't look at him, but she seemed to know it was happening.

"Very mature, love," she commented, tapping her fingers on the file again. "I presume you want to talk to the workers?"

"We will," Shilling nodded.

Bronny nodded in turn, as though giving her permission. Shilling had made it most of the way around the desk now and was half leaning on it again.

"Before we go…" he started slowly. "I do have one more, unrelated, question…"

"Oh?" Bronny raised an eyebrow.

"How long has Julian Silver been working here?"

The Madam thought a moment, seemingly taking a mental tally of all the staff she employed. A look of soft cunning spread across her face.

"Why do you ask?" she grinned.

"Professional curiosity," Shilling replied.

Amy struggled to keep her expression neutral, but she did manage to stay out of the way. All they were doing was questioning each other, yet the tension was viscous. Bronny was looking at Shilling like she was probing him for something. He was as nonchalant as ever.

"How do you know him?" Bronny asked.

"That's my business," Shilling replied.

Bronny grinned openly. "Do you know what his real name is?"

"I do," Shilling nodded.

She motioned at him to continue and spill the gossip.

"His real name is Julian Silver," Shilling stated.

Bronny pulled a face at him. Even Amy didn't believe his answer and she hadn't realised Shilling knew how to lie. He stood resolute and stared Bronny down.

"His real name is Julian Silver," Shilling repeated. "His given name is nobody else's business. Everyone deserves a second chance. I just want to know how long he's been working for you."

"You're sure it's not related to your case?" Bronny checked.

"Positive," Shilling insisted. "Julian wouldn't hurt anyone—" he bit his lip. "Well, he wouldn't kill anyo—*hm.* He would never attack and mutilate innocent women, and he wouldn't help anyone who would either. I'm confident he'd never be the one to start something."

Bronny nodded like she knew what he meant. "He's been with us about a month."

Shilling nodded in reply. It was a polite and reserved nod. It didn't pry, but it was clear he wanted more. Bronny caved before he decided whether to ask for it.

"He only works here part time," she added. "Comes and goes a bit. Very flexible hours, but hard rules. Unusual, but *extremely* popular…" She gave Shilling a probing look. "He's had six proposals already, just this month."

Shilling looked stricken. Amy kept her surprise silent. She didn't realise the investigator swung that way. She hadn't realised he swung any way. Despite his expression, Bronny still looked like she was probing, like she hadn't gotten what she was looking for. Shilling gave her another polite nod and turned towards Amy and the door.

"Charlie…" Bronny called to him, watching him like a hungry hawk. She waited for him to pause, and then softly added, "…he hasn't even looked at them. Threw every single one out without opening it."

Shilling grinned. It was a very smug, very cunning grin on his crooked face. Bronny smiled at him.

"Professional curiosity, huh?" she probed.

"Entirely," he replied with his usual straight honesty.

"Your profession or his?" she coaxed.

"Mine," Shilling answered.

"You'd tell me if you were investigating one of my workers for a crime?" she checked.

"I would," he assured.

Madam Bronny was looking at him like she didn't wholly trust that answer. Amy had reached a point where she felt confused by the whole conversation. The sultry woman behind the desk gave them a dismissive nod, jerking her head at the door like an invitation to leave. Shilling gave her the slightest of grateful bows, imitating respect on his way out, even if he struggled to imply it usually.

He ushered Amy from the office and back into the main room. Their re-entrance was mostly ignored. Conversations had resumed, although some of the groups had shifted. Shilling led the way back into the crowd. Amy peered around curiously for any sign of the man Shilling had been asking about, but he found them first. She felt a looming presence at her shoulder.

"Sleuth!" the dark-haired man threw an arm around Shilling's shoulders. "What are you doing here?"

"I could ask you the same question," Shilling drawled up at him judgementally. "Does Skipp know you're working here?"

"Aye, of course," Julian replied, but his tone was bashful and a nervous blush creeped into his cheeks. "What's it to you?"

"Not much," Shilling shrugged honestly. Julian dropped his arm from around Shilling's shoulders, his exuberance wearing off. Shilling seemed to have that effect on people.

"I need the extra money," Julian stated, trying to hedge the defensiveness in his voice. "It's easy work for good pay."

"Yes, Bronny says you're extremely popular,"

Shilling reiterated. "But turning down the proposals."

Now Julian did blush. "I'm not here looking for a rich spouse," he muttered. "Just trying to save up."

Amy had no idea what was going on anymore, but Shilling seemed very pleased with this development. He motioned to her, changing the subject now that he had what he wanted.

"We're here investigating what happened to Jenny last night, as part of the ongoing case. This is Miss-soon-to-be-Doctor Florin. Florin, this is Julian Silver."

"Doctor Florin is fine," Amy simplified it for the gentleman. "I graduate tomorrow, but Mister Shilling can be a stickler for pedantry, unless it suits him otherwise."

"Can't he just," Julian smirked. "It's a pleasure, Doctor. Congratulations for tomorrow." He took her hand to kiss it. There was a charming, roguish twinkle in his eye as he met her look and brushed his soft lips to the back of her hand. Coupled with his attire, it gave the effect of a lean, half-dressed pirate, and Amy had a sharp inkling into why he may have become abruptly popular.

"Thank you, sir. The pleasure is all mine," she assured.

Julian grinned. It was a very dashing smile. Amy still had no idea what was really going on with Shilling, but if he was interested in Julian, she didn't blame him.

"Actually, Sleuth, I think Skipp mentioned you were a bit stuck with the Jack case," Julian recalled, turning back to Shilling. "Is that what you've brought a doctor along for? You want us all to do some kind of test?" He looked to Amy again and pointed at Shilling. "You seen this guy work, Doc? He does all sorts of weird magic. And I don't just mean card tricks. Charlie here can take scrapings from under someone's fingernails and mix it into these solutions and it changes colour and he can prove where you were and what you were touching. Very impressive."

"Absolutely no magic is involved," Charlie added drily. "Not even with the card tricks."

Amy nodded with a smile. She knew exactly what he was doing, but it wasn't Julian's fault if he'd never studied chemistry. Science could seem quite magical, even when you did know how it worked.

"I'm not here to run any tests," Amy admitted. "Unfortunately, we wouldn't have much to test against. We're just here to ask questions."

"What kind of questions?" Julian asked.

Shilling gave him a surreptitious glance. It was fairly loaded. Amy could see a lot in it, and for a brief second it compounded the confusion, before bursting into clarity. This place was a second home to Shilling. These people were his family. And Julian Silver was a spy. Amy didn't know who for, but Shilling did, and that's why he was curious. He wanted to make sure Julian just needed money from a second job and wasn't spying on people Shilling cared for. Either way, Shilling knew that Julian knew everything that was going on under this roof.

"Like are there any issues with competition in the workplace?" Shilling replied carefully. "Are there any people here who are prone to jealous violence? Any potentially dangerous clients — not necessarily dangerous people themselves, but those who could bring danger with them? Anyone around who might own a hunting knife?"

Julian pursed his lips in thought. Amy glanced around subtly. People were listening. Shilling was trying to be quiet about it, but they were in a public space.

"You really think that Jack of Hearts could be an inside job?" Julian murmured.

Amy and Shilling shared a look. "Not ruling it out," they admitted together.

"Not here," Julian shook his head. "Tensions are running high because of the killings, but no one here would hurt each other. Not like that. Besides, hunting tends to be a pastime of our clients more than our colleagues."

"Hunting knifes aren't hard to come by," Amy replied.

"Aye," Julian agreed. "But any communal weapons of the House will be, uh... made of wood... not sharp. Obviously, everything here is more for theatrical than practical purposes."

"You know all the women are carrying real weapons under their skirts when they go out, Swift," Shilling rebuked him. "I buy the information you sell. Don't lie to me."

"I'm not lying, Sleuth," Julian implored. "Truly, I'm not. I know I haven't been here long, but there's no one here who could do something that awful. No one here would have hurt Jenny. Hell, we didn't even know she was gone! Lizzie was the only one Jenny told. Jen knew the rest of us would have slapped her silly and made her stay if she'd told us she was sneaking out to a job."

"Why the money…?" Amy mused, half to herself as she contemplated the story.

"Lizzie said it was really good," Julian shrugged.

"No, she's right," Shilling pointed at Amy, catching up with her train of thought. "Why the money? Jenny Kent comes from money. She's not wanting in that regard."

"Unless she is?" Amy suggested. "Have you spoken to her parents? Were they cutting her off?"

"Worth looking into," Shilling nodded. "Haven't been by the house yet, given that she wasn't living there. Left that to the police."

"So maybe she did need the money?" Amy mused.

"If she didn't need the money, what was she doing risking her life for that job?" Shilling raised.

"She wouldn't be looking for a spouse here, not unless she wanted to," Amy added. "If everything with the family is as it seems, then she was just here to gain life experience. What kind of experience was she offered that made her take such a phenomenally stupid risk?"

"It can't have just been money…" Shilling rubbed his mouth in thought.

Julian's gaze bounced between them like he was watching a tennis match.

"There… um… there is a certain amount of prestige in the money…" he offered, hesitant to interrupt.

"Does it get competitive?" Shilling asked.

Julian shrugged the kind of shrug that should have

been a nod but people were looking.

"Who was she close to?" Amy asked.

"A few of the girls were close with Jenny," he replied. "But she hadn't really been here that long either. I'd start with Lizzie, being that she was the one Jenny told."

"You think of anything else, Swift, you let me know," Shilling insisted. "I'll pay you to get the information first."

"You ain't paying for this, Sleuth," Julian shook his head. "Anything I hear, I'll make sure to get it to you. Just catch the bastard gutting our girls."

Shilling nodded. He cast his eye about the room. Julian indicated the first door they'd entered through and Shilling gave him another nod before heading off. Amy felt a faint blush rise in her cheeks as she tried for slightly better decorum.

"It was lovely meeting you," she bid him, dipping her head politely.

Julian gave her an utterly dashing grin of agreement, and she felt her blush worsen as she hurried after Shilling. The 'sleuth', as he was dubbed, might have been sure Julian wasn't the Jack, but he was certainly dangerous in other ways. Amy's cheeks were still hot as she followed Shilling back into the entrance hall, contemplating that it simply wouldn't do to be undone by handsome strangers.

Lizzie was back at the front desk. She had composed herself again, but her eyes were bloodshot from crying. She was leaning against the back wall, fidgeting, while the woman who had covered for her perched on the stool behind the desk. Both stopped talking as soon as they had company.

"Hey Charlie," Lizzie sniffed weakly.

"I've been told if I want to know more about Jenny I should speak to you," Shilling raised.

"We were friends with her," the other woman answered far too coldly.

Amy felt alarm bells ring in her mind at the cutting tone.

"This is Olive," Lizzie introduced timidly. "She's new too."

"I'm not that new," Olive retorted. She eyed Amy again as she had when she'd passed them earlier. "Who's your exotic rose, Mister Shilling?"

"Excuse me?!" Amy demanded.

Shilling raised his eyebrows like he knew sparks were about to fly.

"The lady accompanying me is Doctor Florin. She's helping with the case," he answered tactfully. "She came up with an interesting point earlier. If I may inquire, Jenny Kent was from a wealthy family — why was she chasing coins?"

"Because it's human nature," Olive replied cuttingly.

"We wondered if there were any difficulties developing with her parents?" Amy bit back. "If, perhaps, her family were cutting her off? It makes no sense that someone who wasn't desperate for money would take such a foolish risk, given the current circumstances."

"It doesn't make sense, does it?" Olive glowered.

"Jenny said it would be safe!" Lizzie cried. "She said

someone had already died this week and the Jack has never killed two people in a week before!"

"The killings have been increasing rapidly though," Shilling sighed.

"Things were fine between Jenny and her family," Olive insisted. "She didn't need the money. That's not why she went."

"Then why did she go?" Amy asked.

Olive shrugged sourly. She shot a dark look at Lizzie, but Lizzie seemed oblivious in her distress.

"And you know nothing about the person she was meeting?" Shilling pressed. "Obviously there's nothing in Bronny's books, but Jenny didn't think it wise to tell someone where she was going?"

"All we know is that he's rich," Lizzie muttered. "Probably means someone notable, if they're wealthy, but don't know anything else about him. Jenny insisted it be kept very hush, hush."

"Him?" Shilling raised an eyebrow.

"Jenny worked exclusively with male clients," Olive offered, her tone softening. "She was one of those types."

"She said it would be close," Lizzie muttered tearfully. "She… she said she was ducking out for a moment. Just a moment. Just stopping by the inn. She said she wouldn't be long and that it would be safe!"

"And you let her do it!" Olive snapped. "All you had to do was tell someone, Liz! All you had to do was say something and we might have been able to save her! But you didn't. You just thought of yourself."

"I didn't!" Lizzie protested. "She asked me to keep it

a secret!"

"And you thought that was wise?" Olive scoffed. "If I told you I knew who the Jack was but you had to keep it a secret, would you? You're an idiot, Liz, and now Jenny's dead. You were always jealous of her. No one can prove you didn't have a hand in this. What's to say you didn't sell her out to the Jack?"

Lizzie looked like she was about to start screaming. Amy stepped between them, holding out her hands and bidding them calm down. Olive's anger made a lot more sense now. A deep part of Amy could understand it, and grief found all manner of ways to manifest. She knew it was possible that one of the girls was the killer, but Lizzie did not seem likely. Still, she was the only one who might have known where Jenny was going…

"What's the closest inn to this House?" Shilling asked.

"There are a few nearby," Olive admitted. "I don't know which is the closest, but there's the King's Head, the White Swan, and the Three Cups that we used to work from when people didn't want to come here — before we became confined to the House."

"I imagine their businesses are all hurting since this mess," Amy commented.

"A lot of businesses are hurting, ours included," Olive replied. "Our friends are dying. All of London is hurting. Serial killers aren't good for business."

"Although tourism has a nasty habit of picking them up in a rather disturbing way," Shilling remarked, already turning to the front door. His steps were distracted, but they started away from the counter as though to leave.

"Shilling?" Amy called to him.

"Hm?" he looked back. "Oh yes, you two, don't go anywhere. Florin and I might be back later with some more questions. Have a good think about anything Jenny might have told you before she left last night."

Amy resisted the urge to roll her eyes as she left the ladies and hurried after the wayward sleuth. Shilling strolled from the building out into the bright sunshine with Amy right behind him.

"We hadn't finished interviewing them," she pointed out as the door shut in their wake.

"I had," Shilling muttered, fidgeting with his ring. "I know you're late to this party, Miss Florin—"

She resisted the urge to comment on the title of address he chose.

"—but I've been on this case for months now. There isn't much new information to be found. Olive just gave us something new. That's where we're going."

"How so?" Amy asked, following him across the road as they strode away from the High House.

"The inns," Shilling replied. "Most clients of the High Houses come to the Houses themselves to purchase sex. Occasionally, they call out for the workers to come to them, but it's not quite as common. Even rarer, someone will book a separate space that traces back to neither party — usually an inn. Originally, no one could tell me where the dying women were going. The running theory was that they were making house calls but to different residents so no link there. Finally, Bronny tells me that based on the collected information of the Madams they were all going to inns — but can't give me any names. Olive gave me three, and of those three only one is in the right direction, across the park where Jenny's body was found."

Amy gave him a look, or she tried to; he missed it completely. She withheld her sigh and followed him to the White Swan Inn.

# 5

The White Swan Inn was a respectable establishment. Still, Amy felt a flutter of apprehension as she approached the front desk with Shilling. It wasn't the kind of thing he would consider, but it was easy enough to see how the situation could be considered compromising. She was so glad Harry wasn't around to witness it. He'd have conniptions if he knew.

The old, dark, wooden beams of the building were visible, but all the walls were plastered and painted white. They were spotlessly clean and decorated here and there with framed paintings of white swans. Shilling strode straight to the counter and rang the small brass bell. Amy made sure she stood a respectable distance from him. He drummed his fingers on the counter as he waited, tapping his ring in a staccato rhythm.

It didn't matter where they went or what they were doing, he couldn't seem to stop fidgeting. Amy watched his movements, like nervous ticks. He seemed so calm, so disinterested in everything around him, until you watched him closely. She was watching him closely now, trying to work out how he did it. What made him special? She could see him watching the world. As far as she could determine, the reason for his perceived nonchalance was his processing speed. The world of Charles Shilling moved so fast that even his big brain struggled to keep up. He watched all that happened around him, taking everything in, filtering it so quickly his body didn't outwardly express any of it. Not emotionally. The ticks. He tapped his ring on the counter again with a speed that bordered on vibration. She watched the glint on his jittering hand.

"I never took you for a religious man, Mister Shilling," she commented.

He raised his eyebrows at her. Then processed. Her eyes watching his ring. His expression settled as he put it together. It was a thick, heavy signet ring with the symbol of a cross on it.

"I'm not, really. You're correct," he replied. "It was my father's. He was a minister."

"Your father was a minister?" she echoed. To anyone else her tone would have been rude, but she knew he wouldn't care. Implying the apple had fallen far from the tree was the kind of thing Shilling stated outright to people, regardless of feelings, and something he would surely dismiss himself. She wasn't wrong. He shrugged at her.

"Is it such a surprise?" He cocked his head to the side again, that way he did when he was curious. "Rebecca's the responsible, spiritual one. As you can imagine, the books of the Marys' were very popular in our house." He tapped the ring again, but this time watched himself do it, as though aware of the action now. "I kept it because it's the only thing I have left of his. A small piece of sentimentality, I suppose."

Amy watched his sombre face. Shilling had been an object of mild curiosity to her for some years now, ever since his first big case with the police, back when they'd been little more than children. Lord Pound had also been curious about the law working with a boy, but the lad could see things. Some people had thought him psychic or touched by God. Shilling had scoffed at the lot of them. He believed in science, in proving things with cold hard facts, and he'd managed to help the police put away a dangerous killer. To a budding medic that had been a celebratory feat.

He'd quickly become a minor celebrity, as famous for his work as he was infamous for his abrupt personality. She'd only met him a few times, when Henry had seen fit to have him dragged to the house, but she and many others had followed his big cases in the papers. She had also followed, with certain amusement, the papers' failed attempts at an exposé on the reclusive sleuth. Watching him now, it suddenly didn't seem so funny.

"You lost him when you were young?" Amy recalled. "And went to live in the High House?"

"Young-ish," Shilling shrugged. He wasn't meeting her eye, instead scrutinising the swan painting behind the counter. "We were only there for five years. Been out of there now as long as I was in. Still, they were formative years."

Amy did not like the intense curiosity blossoming in her, but she was saved from having to acknowledge it by the arrival of the innkeeper. The disappointment at having her questions halted was carefully bitten down, and she stayed firmly in denial of it. She was here to help solve a murder, not investigate Shilling.

"How may I help you?" the innkeeper asked, blinking at them owlishly.

"I'm Charles Shilling, the detective, and this is my associate, Doctor Florin."

Amy heard a pause before 'doctor', only half a heartbeat long, barely discernible. She tried not to smile as she watched Shilling change her title at whim based on whether or not it would serve him.

"We're investigating the Jack of Hearts killings, and we understand the latest victim was here last night before she died."

Tragedy touched the innkeeper's dark face and he gave a bleak nod.

"I did wonder if someone would come by..." he admitted. "We haven't been in the room since they left. No one's had workers booking rooms for a while, even the men aren't coming out. Room was booked under 'Denarius' but we get a lot of those, and she was clearly working. Whole situation was notable. Then, of course, the morning paper..."

"You didn't send a runner out to the police?" Amy asked.

"To say what?" the innkeeper spread his hands. "They weren't doing anything illegal, and people only come to an inn for business like that if they don't want to be seen. If I dragged the police in on them, no one would ever book with us again."

"But you might have saved her life," Amy sighed.

"What about after she was found dead? Why didn't you contact the police then?"

"Too late to help her then..." the innkeeper answered, shame visible on his face. "And this... it... it's bad for business..."

Amy was prepared to let him know what she thought of business taking precedence when there was a serial killer on the loose, but a look from Shilling paused her before the words formed. His grey eyes turned sympathetically to the man at the counter.

"We get it," he muttered. "Lesser evils and all that."

Neither Amy nor the innkeeper responded to his statement, but the man did look a touch surprised. Shilling shrugged at him as though the situation was obvious.

"You knew there was a connection, that's why you didn't turn down the room," he elaborated. "If the police had come knocking, you didn't want to have destroyed evidence. You didn't want them accusing you of destroying evidence either. But if anyone finds out one of the murdered ladies was here before they died... if you get a name for being 'that place'... well, you're right. Death's bad for business. After the Jack's caught is another matter entirely, but people stop booking if they think a killer might be staying under the same roof. That doesn't put bread on the table, and you have the children to think of."

Amy recognised the astonished blink in the innkeeper's eyes. She wasn't entirely sure she wasn't doing it herself. It was that look people gave when Shilling deduced their reasoning as though reading their minds, except usually better articulated. The moment they realised they really were talking to *that* Charles Shilling. The one from the papers.

There was no argument left to be made. Well, none she was prepared to make. Telling the innkeeper he had been wrong to hide what he knew in the interests of protecting and providing for his family felt churlish. Besides, they were here to solve the case, not debate morals with bystanders.

"Who did the lady meet?" Amy asked instead.

"I never got more than 'Denarius' for the gentleman," the innkeeper admitted. "He was a tall man with a dark moustache in a long black hooded cloak."

Shilling gave the description a sceptical look. "What, like something out of a penny dreadful?" he scoffed.

"Not so ominous as you might imagine," the innkeeper shrugged. "He looked as ordinary as anyone a worker brings here."

"Can we please see the room?" Amy asked.

The innkeeper nodded, taking a key from the wall behind the desk and leading them upstairs. The whole building creaked as they walked up to the second floor. Everything was as clean and neat as downstairs. They were led to the room and the door unlocked for them. Shilling pushed his way in first and Amy followed behind. She wished she could see his face. She wanted to know what he was thinking. It might have helped kickstart her own brain.

The room was so ordinary. There was a sizable bed, neatly made, a large dresser beside the window, and a simple watercolour landscape of the pond at St. James hanging on the wall. Shilling stalked into the room like a cat, edging through the doorway, his narrowed eyes flitting every which way. The first thing he moved towards was the bed. His steps became lower as he entered, melting into a crouch as he eyed the wrinkles in the blankets. Amy followed him slowly. She tried to look the way she knew he did, tried to see things like he did. The sheets were still firmly tucked in both sides.

"Were they even in here…?" she mused.

"They were," Shilling replied, shuffling along beside the bed. "They weren't in the bed but they were on it." He reached out carefully and pulled a single hair from the pillow. The long red curl hung like a loose spring from his fingers. It was a perfect match for the girl Amy had seen in the morgue. Nearly a match for her — the thought crept into her mind as though Madam Bronny had spoken it aloud. She pushed the bleak thought away. This wasn't about her. She couldn't make it about her.

She looked to Shilling, but he was looking at the creases in the blankets and she couldn't meet his eye. His gaze began to flick to her. Her eyes hit the floor. It was an instinctive reaction. A strange panic flared in her chest. She stared down as her cheeks flushed. Why was she blushing?! That was ridiculous. Stop it. Stop it right now. Oh God, her face felt so hot. He was going to start talking about it again. They both knew what had happened in this room, but it wasn't like the murder had happened here, so did it even matter? Would it really help the case?

Something glinted on the floor, just under the valance. She quickly crouched down to pick it up. The metal object slipped against her soft gloves, but she grabbed it and drew it out from under the bed. A dagger. She held it up as she stood again. Shilling moved with her. She wasn't looking at him, but he stood in tandem with her, his gaze on the blade she had drawn from beneath the bed. It was clean. That had to be a good sign. It didn't feel like a good sign.

"What have we here?" Shilling mused.

"I found it half knocked beneath the bed," Amy admitted, looking the dagger over. "This… this here on the handle… that's the Kent coat of arms."

"Jenny Kent's dagger…" Shilling hypothesised. "The girls have all started carrying weapons…"

"But then why didn't she have it with her?" Amy asked. "Why was it under the bed?"

"If she'd been wearing it under her skirt but didn't want to startle her client she might have removed it and hidden it under the bed?" Shilling posed. "The ladies might have started carrying concealed weapons, but they won't be used to them yet. Easy enough to forget."

"No," Amy shook her head. "No, Mister Shilling, if you start carrying a knife in your skirt you don't just forget it." She turned the dagger over in her hands, looking for any clue on it. That was what Shilling did, look at things and spot the little details everyone else missed. All Amy could see was her own scared reflection. She tilted the blade. His face appeared on the other side. He was watching her, doing the little head tilt. Without really knowing why, she stood for a moment just watching his curious face reflecting in the polished blade.

She thought about the last woman who had been in this room, holding this blade. At least Amy was here with Shilling. It might be awkward, but it didn't feel dangerous. Very privately, she was prepared to admit that his curious and crooked face was a little bit sweet. While his tongue could be sharp it never struck with malice, and it was the only part of him with an edge. She pinched her lips together in embarrassment at the memory of Harry and Monty accusing him of murder. Shilling was many things, but Amy was certain he wasn't dangerous. She wasn't the one who needed a dagger.

Something clicked together in her brain. She looked up at him sharply, her eyes meeting his. There was a slight twitch in his expression, as though he'd been expecting this, as though he'd been waiting for it. She realised he had. He was still waiting for her to elaborate on her statement about not forgetting carried knives. In all her life she'd never had a man wait so long for her opinion.

"What if…" Amy began slowly.

The twitch happened again. It was an almost imperceptible nod of invitation to continue. He was hanging on her word.

"What if the moustachioed man is our killer?" she raised.

"Not impossible," Shilling replied. "But not someone obvious or anyone who has any frequent dealings with the Houses — believe me, I've checked—

"

"What if he's a police officer?" Amy interrupted. "A cop, or… or something like that? What if these women are with someone they feel safe around? Someone they feel protected by? Someone they took protection to meet, but then felt safe enough with to consent to being escorted home without protecting themselves from their companion?"

She felt like she was watching Shilling's blood chill. He paled ever so slightly, his brows creasing into a deep glare of concern. The cogs behind his eyes were whirring at the speed of light.

"That would certainly thicken the stew, wouldn't it?" he muttered very quietly. His eyes flicked her way sharply, staring her down. "We may have to take everything we find straight to your father and let him pick the investigators this trickles down to."

"You don't know any officers you trust? What about the lead detective on the case? Detective Rupee?" Amy asked, realising the questions were foolish as soon as she spoke them. Of course Shilling wasn't the type to trust. He shrugged at her.

"I trust Commissioner Farthing, but God only knows if I should," he admitted. "Man has a moustache. Most people have moustaches. Most men. Rupee is a lady without a moustache… but she and I don't get on so well. She's problematically defensive of her institution. If I tried to imply an officer, she'd arrest me again for certain. No… we need to be careful with this…" He stroked his upper lip as though still contemplating moustaches.

"You're not thinking of growing your own, are you?" Amy checked.

"Can't grow facial hair to save my life," Shilling admitted. Amy wasn't surprised. He had rather boyish skin.

"Harry doesn't have a moustache," she added. "Neither does Dad."

Shilling just shrugged at her. She didn't even know why she was arguing the point with him.

"Bag the evidence, Florin," he instructed, digging in his pockets and pulling out a small drawstring cloth bag.

"Right," Amy nodded, taking the bag and stashing the dagger. Her train of thought was slowly derailed as she watched Shilling start to move again. He took tentative steps, shuffling along the side of the bed and sniffing. She didn't even want to ask. He sniffed the pillow.

"Sniff this," he insisted.

Half of her wanted to ask if she had to, but it looked clean and it was in the name of science, for the most worthy cause she could imagine, so she had best suck it up. She leant over and gave the pillow a gentle sniff. Clean and sweet and vaguely perfumed. Nothing notable.

"I don't really smell anything..." she admitted.

"What perfume do you wear, Florin?" he asked.

"Uh..." Amy began.

Shilling pointed urgently at the pillow. "I've been smelling this all over the place recently. Half the dead girls are wearing it. Jenny had this perfume on her body. There are traces of it on this pillow, and I could smell it on her in the park and the morgue. A bunch of the women in Bronny's House have taken to wearing it and they didn't used to. It's the same perfume you're wearing today. Think, Florin! What is it?"

"These women are wearing my perfume?!" Amy blurted.

"Your perfume?" Shilling cocked his head. "Do you make it?"

"What? No. No, I just..." she trailed off. It felt stupid, but at the same time... there was just something so ominous about it all. These women... the similarities...

"It's not about you," Shilling said.

Amy looked up at him. There was a sympathetic slant to his eyebrows and his lips scrunched to the side in a consoling frown.

"I don't mean this to be rude, Florin, but if someone wanted to kill you instead, they would have done it by now. You're perfectly safe. It's just a coincidence."

"I know," Amy sighed, rubbing her brow. "I know... it just... it's uncomfortable how many coincidences are stacking up. The perfume is *rose cannelle* and it's seasonal. Batch made. From a boutique in Soho."

"No time like the present, then," Shilling insisted. "I'll send a message to Farthing to have someone he trusts come down here and talk to the innkeeper, see if we can't get a sketch of the man he saw. You and I will follow our noses!"

He turned to the door and then stopped abruptly. With an almost sheepish expression, he turned back to her.

"Provided you actually want to keep going, of course," he muttered. "Obviously you have more than done your part, if you're uncomfortable with what we're finding... I don't mean to assume..."

"Have we found the killer yet?" Amy demanded.

"We have not," he answered.

"Then I'm not done," she finished.

He did the head tilt. This time it was accompanied by a smile; an endearing, crooked, proud smile. She was growing strangely fond of that smile.

# 6

The afternoon was beginning to grow late, but the perfume store was still open. Charlie let Florin lead the way, even though he could smell it half a block ahead. She was starting to prove herself quite brilliant. Medicine was lucky to have such a bright mind signing up to the cause. Charlie found he liked having someone to talk everything through with, and her theories were sound and logical.

They crossed the threshold into a small store of floor-to-ceiling stained wooden panelling. Even the counter in front of the back wall matched the wood of the room. It was overwhelmingly brown. Most of the walls were covered in neat matching shelves with little glass jars and bottles, all with precise handwritten labels. Charlie felt like his sinuses were being punched. Still, it was better than other overpowering odours his work had brought him into contact with.

The woman behind the counter, who was carefully stashing away a chalk sign, was dressed in browns and yellows. Charlie wasn't sure if it was colour coordination or camouflage. The woman's black hair was bound up in a scarf and frizzed and curled out the top like a fountain. She smiled at them as they came in.

"*Bonsoir,*" she greeted them politely. "We are closing soon, but let me know if you need anything."

"Actually, we need to speak to the owner," Charlie replied.

"*Oui?*" she arched an eyebrow at him.

"My associate and I need to talk to you about purchases of one of your perfumes," Florin said.

Charlie noted the way she stood as she said it. Her posture had always been good, but he suddenly found himself perceiving it, as though she was drawing herself up. She stood tall and regal as she stepped gently across the floor.

"Ah, the Lady Florin," the woman smiled at her directly, suddenly recognising her.

Charlie assumed that was just a matter of attention. Florin was notable. The city was almost certainly full of people who could pick her out of a line up on reputation alone. The woman's eyes rolled over him. He was used to being eyeballed, but not usually like that, and not usually by attractive perfume merchants. He blushed slightly.

"This is not Mister 'Arry Pound though…" she said leadingly in her teasing accent.

It was the first time in his life Charlie had ever been remotely sad that he wasn't Harry Pound. That was a dangerously alien feeling.

"This is Mister Charles Shilling," Amy introduced him with a dismissive wave of her hand. "The detective. He's been aiding father and the law with the Jack of Hearts case."

The merchant's face fell. Charlie was getting used to

that bleak expression whenever the killings were mentioned. It was a normal reaction. At least one of them was having a normal reaction. He wasn't. He could feel a weird, flustered tightness in his chest. It had come to life at the previously comforting notion that he was something far from Harry Pound, and exacerbated when Florin had gestured dismissively at him. Why dismissively? Why was he concerned?

"We were wondering if we could take a look at some of your purchasing lists?" Florin continued. "I know protocol for handing out client information says we should get a letter from my father, which I can do if you need, but —"

"You think I can help Mister Shilling catch the Jack?" the woman interrupted.

"*Oui*, there is a lead that brought us here," Florin nodded. "Actually, it's my perfume. *La rose cannelle*. We want to know who else buys it. Mister Shilling has deduced that a number of the women who have been slain are wearing it when they die."

Now the woman at the counter looked deeply alarmed. Charlie didn't blame her.

"This killer targets women who buy from *my* shop?!" she demanded, pointing at her breast.

"Or purchases it as gifts…?" Florin suggested. "We won't know until we look."

"I don't have addresses, but I do take names of bulk purchases," the woman said. "I have a number of clients from High Houses who purchase from me, but I don't take details for personal sales. Let me get my books." She bustled into the back room and thumped around a moment, before returning with a small stack of ledgers. She untied the leather cords around them and began to leaf through the pages. "Here! *Rose Cannelle*." She pulled a sheet of paper out and turned it around, slamming it down in front of them. "This is everyone who bulk buys this type of perfume from me."

Shilling scanned the list, taking in names and numbers in precise looping handwriting.

"The top name is Harry Pound," he commented.

Florin pulled a face. "That makes sense," she admitted. "I know we buy a lot. I didn't realise we were more than everyone else though." She gave him a look. It was strange, almost apologetic or defensive. "It's seasonal, you see. Hence the bulk purchasing. We get enough to see through the year until the ingredients are in season again. I know it's a bit extravagant…"

"Are you trying to justify standard upper-class behaviour?" Charlie asked, his brow furrowing in confusion.

Florin smiled. It was a wide, genuine smile, all gleaming teeth and crinkled eyes. Even though her gaze dropped, he knew she was smiling at him. It was a curious thing how gentle her smile could be. He wasn't sure how he was triggering it. She smiled at him like he was accidentally entertaining. It was going to require further analysis.

"I suppose I am," she conceded.

"Conventions state that the behaviour of the hegemony need not be justified," Charlie muttered gloomily.

Florin's smile widened. She found him amusing.

That was something. It was strange though. Very strange. Charlie was used to being laughed at. He didn't feel like Florin was laughing at him. She clearly was, but there was nothing malicious about it. She wasn't having her fun at his expense. It seemed to come from a place of fondness. Charlie could count on one hand the number of people who could be described as fond of him. If what he saw in her expression was real, perhaps he was going to need another hand.

"We… uh… we can just copy down these first ten names here," he muttered, steadfastly disapproving the heat rising in his cheeks. He pulled a small notepad and a pencil from his pocket and hunched over the counter, scribbling down a copy of the merchant's notes. "Then we can take the list to Bronny and run the perfume buyers against her House clients. See if anything pops out to her. If she can't narrow our list further, we'll just have to look into everyone."

"You can leave Harry off," Florin volunteered helpfully.

Charlie ignored her and wrote Harry's name down anyway. He wasn't trying to be rude, and he knew that Harry's purchase had already been justified. There was a perfectly reasonable explanation. Charlie was fairly sure there was a perfectly reasonable explanation for leaving Harry's name on the top of the list too, even if it had nothing to do with the Jack. He didn't want to do much psychological digging into what it might be, but he had a niggling suspicion it had something to do with finding out what Bronny might say about Harry. Florin had been adamant in the morgue, and maybe she was fooling herself, but Charlie wasn't stupid, and Harry wasn't a virgin. Bronny's house was the closest to the Pounds. Charlie wasn't much of a betting man, but he could put two and two together.

He finished scribbling down his notes and pocketed the list. When he looked up, the merchant was smiling at him. It was a mysterious, knowing smile that made him blush harder.

"Thank you for your help, Ma'am," he dipped his head politely to her.

"You tell me what you find," she instructed. "If one of my clients is killing those girls, let me know. I will poison them before they can kill again."

"That's... extremely illegal and moderately immoral," Charlie replied. "But when we find the Jack we will hand them over to the police before they can kill again."

The women shared a look Charlie couldn't translate.

"If you think of anything else, let me know," Florin bid the woman.

She nodded in return. "Anything I can do. My husband is walking me home from the shop every night now. It's nice, but I wish it wasn't occurring under such dire circumstances. I'm terrified to go out alone."

"You have the benefit of not being an escort," Charlie shrugged at her. "There is a strong argument to be made that anyone who isn't a sex worker is safe from the Jack. Still, you are a striking woman and other ladies who fit your physical profile are counted amongst the dead."

The merchant raised an eyebrow at him again and turned to Florin.

"Are all his compliments that backhanded?" she asked.

"You start to get used to it," Florin smiled.

Shilling looked between them, but they seemed to be having a conversation with their eyes that he wasn't privy to. He shrugged.

"Just stating facts…" he mumbled.

Florin smiled that smile again, and Charlie felt a horrible anxiety tickle his stomach. It was nauseating.

"*Merci pour votre temps,*" Florin thanked the merchant once more and headed for the door.

Charlie hurried out after her. He didn't want to get 'the look' again.

The sun was setting a strong peach through the smog and it lit the sky like a coral wonderland. Charlie watched the world hurry by. He cocked his head to the side as he took everything in. The after-work rush was trying to get home before dark. He could see a number of people hurrying along. Higher levels of anxiety than normal. That was expected. Some strode purposefully and confidently through the street as though they had nothing to fear. Some scurried along like they were praying for invisibility. Charlie watched both kinds in equal measure. He saw three crimes being committed, but only one of them was something he actually disapproved of.

Florin was watching him. He didn't know what to do about that. She looked at him like she knew something about him that he didn't know, and it made his chest feel tight and funny. He felt like he needed to loosen his collar, but knew it wouldn't do any good.

"So now we take that list back to Madam Bronny?" she asked.

"It's getting late," Charlie squinted at the sky. "I'll walk you home, then I can drop the list off on the way back to my place. Bronny can look it over tonight and we can— oh, well, I can check back with her tomorrow. You have graduation."

"You're going to walk me home?" she grinned.

"Of course," he replied in confusion. "With everything that's going on I can't well let you walk alone."

"Why, Mister Shilling?" she teased. "Am I also a striking woman who fits the profile?"

He stared at her like she'd gone mad. He could tell she was teasing, but he didn't understand the joke. It felt in bad taste, but that seemed out of character for so intelligent a person, so perhaps there was something he was missing.

"Yes," he stated, head cocked and perplexed. "You are an attractive woman who fits the profile, Florin. We've had that discussion today — touched on it multiple times, in fact. You expressed concern about it earlier. Even if you hadn't, it would be inappropriate for me to abandon you now so close to dark. So, I intend to walk you home, unless you have any strong objections. I will hear you out if you do."

She was smiling at him, that damn bewildering smile that just seemed to know so much and grow with every word he said. He felt like he'd accidentally fallen into a world where he was a comedian.

"You know, Mister Shilling," Florin began in a

demure tone that alarmed him. "Despite your reputation, you're really rather chivalrous."

"Well, despite its reputation, chivalry is not only the domain of the nobility," Charlie replied. "Recent family elevation aside, being born as I was does not make me a brute."

Florin laughed. A hot flush crept up Charlie's neck at the sound. Anyone else he knew would have turned their nose up at his tone. His sisters would have despaired at him, but Amy Florin laughed, and she smiled, and then she tucked her hand in his elbow.

"Quite," she agreed. "I rather think, Mister Shilling, that in every way that actually counts, you're really a gentleman."

Charlie stayed frozen for a moment. He was worried his arm was about to catch fire where Florin held him, and the cogs of his brain had become stuck on her phrasing. The implication of her words... it sounded like something he'd say. *In every way that actually counts.* His throat seemed to have swollen shut and he had no way of forcing his revelation out. Florin didn't seem to have noticed that he couldn't speak.

"Shall we?" she asked.

Still unable to form words, and hoping that the sunset was hiding the actual colour of his face, he gave a nod and led on. The fear of combustion from the intense heat radiating from her gloved hand tucked against his sleeve had not dissipated, but he didn't want her to remove it either.

As they came to the first street corner, a small crowd was gathered around a girl peddling copies of the evening paper. Charlie glimpsed the headline as they passed by. 'LONDON CURFEW?' took up a large section of the page with 'IN THE WAKE OF THE JACK OF HEARTS MURDERS'— stamped underneath and cut off by the folded page.

"His Lordship's been busy," Charlie commented, almost forgetting his anxiety.

"I'm not surprised they're talking about it again," Florin sighed. "Daddy's not used to feeling helpless, and he doesn't like it. If he must lock people in their homes to keep them safe, he will."

"They haven't made a call yet," Charlie pointed out, remembering the question mark. "There are consequences they don't want to have to deal with. You know the only reason they're making such a fuss is because the women dying are high-class sex workers," he muttered. "I'm all for everyone getting the protection and care they deserve, but if the Jack was targeting poor women, the House of Lords would all be wringing their hands and sighing that there was nothing they could do."

"That's beneath you, Shilling," Florin criticised.

"It's beneath basic human decency," Shilling muttered. "It's still true. You know it is. If it were working girls on street corners, or maids, or bakers, or anyone who had to work for a living yet barely scrape by, you know the Lords wouldn't care, but it's their daughters and sisters and escorts dying so they're talking about locking down the city."

She was watching him again, but there was no judgement in her eyes. He appreciated that, even if he didn't know how to tell her so. She knew he was right. The powerful took care of their own, but it didn't trickle down. He knew Florin was smart enough to see it. Some of her comments hinted at such. She just wasn't going to agree with him too loudly because her family were 'proper' and he was a 'menace' and an 'anarchist'. It was better than being called complicit.

They turned into the back alleys, taking a shortcut away from the main crowds. The faster he could get Florin home, the faster he could go back to life as normal. Whether or not he wanted it, it was inevitable. She was dragging her steps. He didn't blame her. He enjoyed what he did too, and he wouldn't want to give it up for her life. Maybe, if he got stuck again, he could come back and knock on her door once she was done graduating. Subtly. Give her the option of staying involved without her having to ask. He knew she wanted to. He could feel the question hovering about her. She was dying to ask him something. It wasn't like he hadn't enjoyed the help.

"Mister Shilling…?" Florin started slowly.

"Of course, Florin," he sighed, feeling strangely elated.

"Well, I was just wondering… how you know?" she continued.

"It's obvious," he shrugged.

"Is it?" she gave him a curious look. "How so? How do you always know when someone's lying? Is it a trick?"

He paused, in thought and pace, and took stock. They were not on the same page, nor the same book. He came to a full griding halt as his brain threw its own book out the window, picked up hers, and turned to the right page. Florin paused as well, her fingers coming together in front of her and fidgeting.

"I was thinking about everything you said earlier," she elaborated. "I want to know how you always know when people are lying. You say it's obvious, but, really, I mean... how? How can you be so sure?"

"Oh, well..." he frowned slightly as he thought. "I don't know for sure when everyone's lying. I've been tricked before. But most people... well... they have tells, don't they? A great many tells are universal — tiny expressions we all convey unconsciously without realising it... and, of course, there are the lies people tell that don't make any sense, they just haven't realised it."

"You accused us all of lying in the morgue today," she recalled.

"You were all lying in the morgue," he muttered, starting to walk again. Florin trailed after him.

"Why are you so sure?" she pressed.

Charlie sighed loudly. This was not a conversation he wanted to have. He'd tried to stay out of it earlier, but they'd dragged him in then and all he'd gotten for it was a scolding. She wasn't going to like his answers any better now.

"It's none of my business, Florin," he sighed. "Let's just leave it at that."

"How did you know I'm not looking forward to the wedding?" she blurted.

"What, you think you're doing such a good job of hiding it?" He cocked his head sarcastically at the alleyway before him, continuing to stride ahead of her while she chased after him.

"Yes, actually, I do," she insisted.

Charlie sighed again. "Pound Junior is not smart enough for you, Florin. You very clearly love him, but you just as clearly are not in love with him. You seek challenge — no one goes into medicine if they want a boring life where they are happy with how things are. Medicine is where breakthroughs in science and technology are born. It is where revolutions happen. That is what you chose for yourself. Harry Pound is what was chosen for you, and it doesn't get more dull and predictable than a Lord's son worshiping the crown of the aristocracy that gives him power. Of course you don't want to marry him."

"What if I wanted stability at home to balance the excitement and trauma of work?" she asked.

"Then he'd be a better match for you," Charlie replied. "Pity you don't. Look, Florin, it's none of my business. I cannot emphasise that enough. I'm not exactly the person people come to for relationship advice, all right? Lost your cat? I can find them. Lost the love that once burned in your heart? Best take that one up with God. It sounds like her area of expertise."

"What if I never had it...?" she muttered.

Charlie did his very best not to care, and failed utterly. Whenever Florin got uncomfortably honest with him she said things that sounded like the echoing depths of his conscious. He knew what she meant. What if she didn't love? What if she was broken? He hadn't found the answer to those questions yet. Not for himself or anyone else.

"I am not the person to be asking about that," he insisted softly.

"But you're the only one who knows…" she pleaded. "And I didn't even have to tell you. I've never told anyone. Not even Laura and Jane. But you know, you just knew, without me even having to say anything. You were right. I love Harry. I love him like a brother. The Pounds are the only family I've ever known… but…"

"You never told your friends?" Charlie mused. "Interesting. I thought they knew."

"Really?" Florin seemed surprised.

Charlie shrugged. "I was eavesdropping on a farce. It was hard to tell where the rubbish stopped and started."

"Oh really?" Her tone became sharper.

He pulled a face, obliviously. "The three of you were nattering on about Harry being squeamish, which is about as honest as him waiting for marriage—"

"Excuse me?!" Florin demanded.

Charlie raised an eyebrow at her and tilted his head. She was glaring at him.

"He goes white as a sheet at so much as a papercut," she insisted. "And I would know if he… if he was…"

"Oh, like you?" Charlie prodded. "Pontificating about your patience with your friends like the three of you weren't experimenting and fingering each other in college? Ugh—!"

Florin slammed her hand over his mouth and pinned him to the wall so hard his shoes barely touched the ground.

"Mister Shilling!" she hissed near his face, like a fox about to bite it off. "You are going to pretend you never said that and then you will never say anything like it for the rest of your life. Do I make myself clear?"

Shilling half-nodded with her glove still clamped firmly over his mouth. He had an excellent view of muddy green eyes, full of murder. Florin had a spray of black freckles across her walnut skin that looked like ebon stars. There was a slight gap between her front teeth. Her whole face was scrunched with homicidal warning. He couldn't stop staring at her. Something very weird had happened to his breathing, but it seemed to have less to do with her hand on his mouth and more to do with how closely she had him pinned to the wall. Charlie didn't usually get this close to anyone, except for the occasional fight. He was not going to fight her. Although, he wasn't sure he wanted her to let him go either.

"Mister Shilling," she continued in the same deadly tone. "You are not allowed to say things like that about people. It is deeply inappropriate. For your sake, as well as everyone else's, take better care with your words." She let him go, dropping him slowly and stepping back.

"Understood," he muttered, but the word got mangled on the way out, so he cleared his throat and tried again, more forcefully. "Understood, Miss Florin."

He watched her step back from him as he brushed down his coat. He didn't know why he bothered. She hadn't actually mussed him at all. Still, he felt deeply mussed. There was something troubled in her expression. She wasn't happy with what she had just done, but she hadn't been happy with what he had said either. This was why he didn't get involved.

"And it's not… It doesn't…" she muttered so softly it was barely audible.

Charlie rolled his eyes. "You're a doctor, Florin. Please don't try and tell me it doesn't count."

He turned to continue, and she fell in step with him. He could feel the words hovering about her.

"I've had idiots do that," he warned her. "People try and tell me that it doesn't count. That biologically my sisters are and shall remain delicate little virgins." He shook his head. "None of them have ever had to listen to Susan scream, I assure you."

Florin raised an eyebrow at him.

"What?" he muttered.

"Lady Guinea's a screamer?" Florin questioned teasingly.

"You have no idea…" Charlie grumbled.

Florin laughed at him. At least one of them found it amusing, and it helped to settle the mood again to have her giggling at him. He liked her laugh, and her smile, which was an unsettling feeling. He didn't even know her. Well, he barely knew her. Okay, he knew her better than most people, but he'd only really spent a single day in her company so he felt like he shouldn't know her at all. God, feelings were stupid. He picked up the pace again. The sun was still setting, and he'd rather get her home before dark if he could. The mood settled again as she started dragging her heels. He couldn't force her home.

"You really think Harry's unfaithful?" she asked softly.

Charlie wanted to throw himself off a bridge to avoid the conversation, but there wasn't anything convenient nearby. He settled for rolling his eyes.

"I'm sorry, Shilling. I didn't mean to lash out before. I was just startled," she murmured, shuffling along beside him through the streets. "I just... I've never talked to anyone about this before. I want to know what you think. Really, I do."

The energy radiating from her was imploring, and it made him feel weak. God, it was awful. Utter discombobulation.

"If he's anything like you..." Charlie began carefully, "he will be trying to manage the situation with the same care and grace you've shown. The two of you are unusual. You're betrothed, but you grew up in the same house, with the same father. One can see the origin of the discomfort bloom with ease. Like I keep trying to say, Florin, it's really none of my business."

"It would be if I got you to look into Harry's gambling and you dug something up..." she hinted.

"You want to hire me?" Charlie tilted his head.

"Would you take the job?" she asked.

"I have no idea..." he answered honestly, trying to weigh up the pros and cons in record time. "I have to catch the Jack before I take on anything else."

"Of course," Florin nodded. "Will you keep me apprised of the case?"

"Even if I said no, you could make his Lordship insist," Charlie sighed.

"But I wouldn't," she replied with that abrupt honesty he found so endearing. "I'm asking you, Shilling, and will respect your answer. The same way you respected everything I said today. I'm sorry I can't go with you to Bronny's and help more tomorrow. I think Daddy and Harry would have me committed if I tried to skip graduation. However, we're having a party tomorrow evening. A dinner party. Would you consider attending as my guest? You could bring me up to speed on everything you find."

Charlie wasn't quite sure where the cobbles were anymore. His feet were still functioning, one boot in front of the other. Except he couldn't feel the ground. Something important had come detached in his brain. He really hoped that wouldn't be a problem.

"I will see where the case takes me," he answered carefully, fidgeting with his ring. "But I will certainly consider stopping by unless a strong lead takes precedence."

"That's all I can ask for," she smiled and stopped.

He nearly walked straight past her front gate. That had been quick. His head was so hazy he barely knew where he was. This was a disaster. Maybe it was something he'd been sniffing in the perfume shop that had addled his brains. Maybe it was something in Florin's perfume that addled people's brains! That was why the killer gave it to the victims! No, that didn't make any sense, and Florin's brain wasn't addled. Oh no, he was going mad.

"It was a privilege to work with you today, Mister Shilling," she nodded to him. "Thank you for letting me tag along."

"You did more than tag along, Florin," Charlie assured. "It's a pleasure to have a keen mind keeping pace with my own for a change. Your insights regarding the body and perfume have hopefully won us some good headway and saved some time — maybe even another life."

She smiled at him and held out her hand. He shook it politely. Her glove was soft but her fingers felt cold. Maybe he was just running hot. Maybe there wasn't much of a maybe about it.

"Good luck for tomorrow," he said.

"And you, Shilling." She squeezed his hand. "If anyone's going to catch this evil bastard, it's you."

"You… really believe that, don't you?" Charlie muttered, meeting her eye.

"I really do," she insisted, letting go of his hand and turning to walk through the gate.

He watched her walk away, an art piece of burgundy curls and matching skirts sashaying up the stairs to the front door. Charlie was aware that he was nervously nibbling the side of his bottom lip and unable to stop himself. She didn't look back. He didn't expect her to. Thank God she didn't, or she would have seen how worried he was. She thought he could do this. That must mean she had seen something today that inspired that confidence. He wished he knew what. The best theory they had right now had been hers. He needed to solve the case. The need had been consuming him for six months. Maybe Florin was the one who actually could.

Except he knew if he chased after her, if he banged on the door and asked how she knew, she'd just laugh at him. She'd laugh that same helpless and enamoured laugh she'd done several times today. The one that seemed to suggest there were very obvious things he was missing but was followed with no useful explanations.

He sighed and flicked his fingers between his coat buttons and signet ring, looking for something comforting to stim. Eventually, his hand settled for the folded suspect list in his pocket. He scuffed the thick corner of creased paper under his thumb nail soothingly as he turned down the street and strode off.

# 7

Amy hurried through the front door and fell back against it, snapping it shut behind her. She stared at the ceiling, willing her heart to slow as she took deep soothing breaths. Someone was watching. She looked over at the thick grey eyebrow raised her way.

"Hello Digby," she smiled.

"Good evening, Miss," the butler gave her a nod. "We were expecting you back earlier. Glad to see you safe."

"Thank you," she grinned breathlessly, still not moving from the door. She turned her head, but didn't dare peek out the windows either side. "Digby, is there a man at our gate?"

"He just walked away," Digby growled. "Do I need to make sure he's kept away?"

"No! No, no, no, not at all, no, no…" Amy shook her head. She was still saying no. She didn't seem to be able to stop. "No, he's completely fine."

Digby's eyebrow shot up again.

"I'm starting to sound a bit like a madwoman, aren't I?" she tempered her rambling.

"There's certainly an unusual cadence," Digby

admitted. "Are you all right, Miss?"

"I've had the most bizarre day…" Amy confessed.

Footsteps sounded on the landing. She looked up the stairs. Harry came to an abrupt stop when he saw her. So did her euphoria. A thousand thoughts flashed through her head at once. The predominant sensation was guilt.

"Amy!" Harry cried at the sight of her. "Where the hell have you been? We've been worried sick!"

"I was out helping with the case," she replied.

"What? At the morgue?" he countered. "All this time?"

"No…" she admitted. "No, I went with Mister Shilling to investigate a few leads after the morgue."

Most of the time Harry was handsome enough that she could fool herself into believing everyone's lie, but even if that hadn't been proving difficult today, when he was this angry there was a violent fire in his eyes that scared her. He'd never hurt her. Harry wasn't that kind of person. Still, sometimes his eyes could get dark and frightening. She could see him clenching his jaw to keep the words back.

"I'm sorry I'm late, Harry," she apologised softly. "I didn't mean to scare you."

He stood at the railing, his lips twitching as he tried to settle his nerves. Silence reigned in the space of his calming breaths.

"Come up to dinner," he invited once he could get his tone calm and even again. "You can tell us all about it."

She nodded, but he didn't wait to see it. Amy

watched painfully as Harry stalked up the stairs. She hadn't meant to upset him. However, if the options were upsetting Harry and catching the killer or pleasing Harry and letting the Jack escape… she would donate him her entire handkerchief collection and walk out the door. Lives were at stake, which meant this was bigger than one man's feelings.

She followed him upstairs to the dining room, trailing a safe distance. Henry was already standing by the door when she came in.

"Amy, darling!" He threw out an arm and caught her by the shoulders, kissing her cheek. "You're not getting dressed for dinner?"

"She's already late," Harry sniped, standing away from them.

"Well, someone's in a mood…" Henry glared warningly at his son.

"It's all right, Daddy," Amy kissed his cheek in return, daintily avoiding his scratchy whiskers. "I'm sorry for holding you up. I didn't mean to scare you."

"Oh, we're all right, precious," he soothed her, motioning to the table that they should all be seated. "Come and tell me what you found."

They all moved as he bid. Harry didn't take his usual seat at her side, instead seating himself deliberately opposite her. It was the same chair Shilling had sat in that morning. She wondered if he was trying to make a point, and felt a faint fluttering of alarm when she realised she didn't care.

As the food was brought out, she confessed in hushed tones that Shilling was still following a strong lead and that they had a couple of compelling theories to investigate — namely, the bone-chilling notion that the Jack might work in law enforcement.

"Lady Mary in Heaven, tell me you jest…" Henry muttered.

"It would explain a lot of why they have been so difficult to catch," Amy replied. "If they know the processes of investigation, they will know a lot of what to avoid. They might even be deliberately covering up or corrupting evidence. But it's just a theory for now. We have to follow the evidence first. This theory doesn't leave this room! Understand?"

"You spend one day with him and suddenly it's an entire conspiracy…" Harry glowered, pushing his food around his plate. "Now the police are helping cover for the killer."

"Don't put words in my mouth, Harry," Amy warned. "This is just about the Jack. They must be someone who makes these women feel safe, otherwise the ladies wouldn't risk it. This is just one theory, but when we were at the High House today —"

"When you were where?!" Harry exclaimed.

Everyone froze. Amy paused mid-sentence, pressing her lips together as she tried to work out how to back out of what she had just walked into. Harry was staring at her across the table like she'd admitted to gutting a pig.

"You went to a High House with Charles Shilling?!" The accusation and contempt in his voice was palpable.

Amy felt a blush blossom hot and red, intensifying the longer he stared at her. It was ridiculous. She had nothing to be embarrassed about. Nothing! Yet her face kept growing hotter. She felt like her cheeks were redder than her skirt. Henry gave her a sly look.

"Educational experience, was it?" he teased, breaking the tension.

"Daddy!" Amy scolded him, slapping his arm with her napkin. "It was for the investigation!"

"So you didn't peruse the wares…?" Henry joked.

Amy felt like she was going to spontaneously combust. The memory of Shilling and his interest in the dashing Julian lit a fire of embarrassment inside her. It was none of her business, but he was far too handsome to pretend she hadn't noticed.

"I barely saw anything," she replied primly, trying to cover her embarrassment. "We spoke to the Madam and a couple of Jenny's grieving friends. That's all."

"And it didn't bother you to go?" Harry huffed. "You didn't think it inappropriate to accompany Shilling there? To be seen stepping out with him?"

"Excuse me?!" Amy rounded on him. "To be what?!"

"Harry!" Lord Pound scolded.

"I'm just saying," Harry shrugged defensively.

"You certainly are, and I would warn you to take care, boy," Henry scolded.

"After what you said to her?" Harry snapped back.

"Mine was harmless teasing," Henry defended stiffly. "We both know our Amelia, and she is a picture of professionalism. I do not imagine that she conducted herself with anything less than the utmost respectability today, and I do not know what got up your nose to imply otherwise."

"Thank you, Daddy," Amy murmured to him.

Henry gave her a reassuring nod. Harry was glaring at both of them. Amy met his glare. He could barely hold it when she actively tried to outstare him. His face was pale, pinched. Hurt.

"This isn't about me," Amy said. "Why does he bother you so, Harry?"

"It is about you," Harry replied. "Shilling is a freak and a lunatic—"

"Harry!" Lord Pound barked.

"He is! He is, father, and it bothers me that neither of you can see that!" Harry exclaimed. "That neither of you are concerned about the social implications of being seen with him. You said you would help him at the hospital, Amy, and God herself knows I tried to understand that... but then you went off with him for the day?! You went to a High House with him?! What were you thinking?! When you didn't come home this afternoon I started to worry something had happened! What if he'd kidnapped you? Stuffed you in a sewer to hide your body? Trapped you down in his basement to perform hideous experiments on you?"

"Jesus Christ, Harry..." Lord Pound rubbed his brow wearily.

"He does it!" Harry defended. "I've heard about it! He keeps all kinds of weird experiments in Lady Guinea's basement!"

"Good God, Harry..." Amy shook her head, unconsciously mimicking Henry. "You know, you should have come with us today after all. We could have used someone on the case with your imagination."

"My imagination…" Harry scoffed.

"Yes, Harry, imagination," she snapped. "He's harmless! Whatever personal dislike you have of Shilling, that is your problem, but having spent more time with him today than you ever have, I can tell you with the utmost confidence that he is quite brilliant and a perfect gentleman. In fact, I invited him to the graduation dinner tomorrow."

Harry looked like she'd slapped him. Amy didn't care. She didn't know what was going on with him, but she was sick to death of it. Henry had raised an eyebrow at her.

"You invited him to the party tomorrow?" Lord Pound echoed.

"I did," Amy replied haughtily. "Because he's still out there working the case, while I have to come home because God forbid I'm late for dinner!"

"Amy…" Henry warned.

"And then tomorrow I can't help either," she continued cuttingly. "Because I have to dress up in stupid robes and go to a stupid ceremony and have a stupid party while other people risk their lives to catch this monster! So, yes, Daddy, I told him that he ought to come tomorrow evening and let us know what he finds."

"Tell us how you really feel…" Henry drawled, looking at her from under his bushy eyebrows.

"I think she just did," Harry stated coldly.

"The day before you graduate is an unfortunate time to decide you no longer want to pursue medicine," Lord Pound commented.

"It's not that," Amy sighed. "I didn't mean… I'm sorry. Graduation isn't stupid… I just… I wanted to be a doctor so that I could help people. I wanted to save lives. Now, something very real and very awful is killing people, and… and it's terrifying. I feel so helpless… but… but Shilling… what he's doing is comforting. It's inspiring. He's fighting back against the murderer the same way I wanted to be able to fight back against disease and infection."

"That's a very sweet way of looking at it, darling," Henry smiled.

Amy could see a softness in his expression. He thought her naïve, but didn't consider that a weakness. Not like Harry, who looked like he'd been slapped, and stood from the table. Amy didn't deign to comment.

"No one excused you, boy," Henry warned.

"Well, you're going to have to," Harry declared. "I told John I'd meet him at the club tonight and, unlike some people, I don't want to keep anyone waiting."

"Harry!" Lord Pound barked at his son.

"What?" Harry was still looking at Amy, his eyes full of challenge. "I thought Amy was warming to disrespectful behaviour."

Her eyes shot up to him. She met the challenge in his look. How dare he?! He was so angry. Good. He deserved to be, after that outburst. She'd felt so guilty downstairs when she realised she'd upset him, but this was barbaric. She felt like she'd been listening to Harry be rude about Shilling all day. The irony was so bitter she could taste it. Sharing the bitterness was only fair.

"You know what the difference is, Harry?" Amy sat

back in her chair and looked up at him, heat still prickling her cheeks but fire sparking behind her ribs. "When Shilling's rude it's never malicious. That's why he's endearing and you're boorish."

Silence reigned. She picked up her knife and fork again, turning to her plate with casual dismissal of him.

"Go see your friends, Harry, just remember to check your attitude on the way out," she said.

He was frozen, but she wasn't going to acknowledge him again. He didn't deserve it. She wanted him to leave, to go somewhere else and think about what he'd said. When he broke, it was jerky and uncomfortable, as though he was reeling. The way he walked from the room was a near stagger, but Amy was still hurting so she called out after him.

"And maybe your wallet!"

He didn't turn back, and the final jab was deeply satisfying... provided she never looked up and met Henry's eyes. She could feel his warning gaze boring into the side of her face. It was going to be impossible to ignore forever. Very slowly and timidly, she turned to him. It was exactly the look she'd been expecting, and she knew she'd earnt it.

"That was rude," Henry chided.

"He started it!" she protested.

"Perhaps, but two wrongs don't make a right, precious," he cautioned. "What has gotten into you two?"

"I don't know," Amy admitted. "I'm sorry, Daddy. I really don't know. I... Why does Harry hate Shilling so much?"

"I could hazard some guesses, but they'd be as good as yours," Henry sighed. "Amy, darling, Harry loves you. I know you two don't always see eye-to-eye, but I know that there is no one in the world he cares about as much as you. He doesn't want to see you getting hurt, and he doesn't want you spending time with people he doesn't trust. I'm glad you're getting on well with Mister Shilling, but let's not pretend that boy is normal. Charles Shilling is an odd little duck. As proud as I am that you want to help him, and I am so proud, Amy, I mean this with all my love, precious, you're a junior doctor at best. You're utterly brilliant, but you're not a practiced investigator. Maybe this one you help where you can and leave the rest to the professionals?"

Amy sat in silence for a moment, letting her thoughts whirl. Henry took the silence as quiet acquiescence. He reached out and patted her hand comfortingly. Her lips parted, as though to whisper the rearing thought, but she pressed them shut again and kept it to herself.

Shilling thought she was smart enough. He had said it was nice to have a mind around that was sharp enough to keep up. The Pounds were her family and they loved her, but they still saw her as a little girl that needed protecting. Shilling saw her as a medical professional with a keen mind and a sharp wit who could keep pace with him. Telling Henry that wouldn't help though. Telling Harry would probably have blown the roof off the dining room. Still, every ounce of excited wind had been sucked from the sails of graduation, and the only faint breeze on her horizon was the thought that Shilling might come by tomorrow evening with a puzzle to solve.

It was late. Bronny's office was dimly lit with soft orange light from multiple lamps. Charlie was seated at the desk, fast asleep with his head on the corner. He was snoring quietly and drooling a little. His hair was a mess and he looked like he'd crawled in off the street. The Madam watched him fondly as his shoulders rose and fell. She shut the ledger quietly and reached out a hand, stroking his hair down and trying to settle the spray of blonde straw escaping across the polished mahogany.

"Charlie...?" she murmured.

"M'wake!" he startled, half-falling off the side and barely catching himself.

"Rough night last night, love?" she asked.

"Rough night, long day..." he muttered, twisting and stretching his back. He surreptitiously wiped the small puddle with his sleeve and scrubbed his cheek with his cuff. "How's the list going?"

"Nothing on my end," she sighed. "But I can run it by the other Madams and see what comes back."

"Appreciated," Charlie muttered, rubbing the grit from his eyes. "I don't know if it's a long shot or not... but Florin helped me think out some new concepts today, so anything that redirects my brain is a good thing. I still feel like I'm standing in Trafalgar Square lamenting my inability to find the Eiffel Tower."

"You can't be that far off, Charlie," Bronny assured. "But I take it we should have gotten you a pretty assistant years ago?"

"She was never my assistant," Charlie replied. "Florin more than proved herself my equal, if not my superior, at the morgue today. It's a pity her intellect is unintentionally inhibited by her family. Now she's taking your advice and keeping safe." He paused and rubbed his face again. "She said I can go and talk to her again if I get stuck. Said she wants to be kept in the loop…"

"Did she now?" Bronny watched him like he was a scruffy puppy.

"Yes," Charlie replied, cocking his head to the side in confusion. "Why did you say it like that?"

"Why did you, Charlie?" she smiled.

His head tipped further, as though trying to see her remark from a different angle. Bronny's smile deepened at the confusion on his face.

The door opened sharply and they both turned towards it.

"You knock before you enter, Mister Silver," Bronny warned the brooding dark figure in her doorway.

"This can't wait," Julian replied. "Lizzie's missing."

"What do you mean 'missing'?" Bronny echoed.

"I mean we've searched this place top to bottom, and we can't find her," he answered. "I told you I had to break up that tiff between the lasses earlier, there was some finger pointing about Jenny. Looks like Lizzie's done a runner."

"When?" Charlie demanded, standing and patting

his pockets.

"We dunno for sure," Julian admitted. "Might've just missed her. Might've been gone an hour."

"I'm on it," Charlie assured.

"Go with him, Silver," Bronny insisted. "Drag that girl back by her hair if you have to. I will release her from service in the morning, if that's what she wants, but Hell will freeze over before another of my ladies is killed under the cover of darkness."

"Aye," Julian nodded.

Charlie was already brushing past him. Julian turned with him and followed at his shoulder. They shot up the hallway from the back room and hit the street in seconds. Julian straightened his collar as he watched Charlie pause on the front steps. The sleuth's pale coat, face, and hair reflected the lamplight like he was on fire, and it flashed in his colourless eyes as they narrowed at the landscape.

"This way," he instructed, heading up the street.

He zipped away and Julian hurried to keep pace with him. He was taller, with longer strides, but Charlie could take off like a terrier and Julian didn't always know where he was going. The paths he followed did not inspire confidence. Charlie moved with purpose, pausing rarely, which only unsettled Julian further. They wound through tight alleyways. These were the last places either of them wanted to think about Lizzie travelling through.

"She's heading for the park," Charlie muttered, picking up speed.

"How do you know?" Julian called after him.

Charlie didn't answer and Julian kept chasing. They broke out into the street running along the park fence. The railings were high and pointed, turning into a gate at the far end of the street and a stone wall close by. If it hadn't been close they wouldn't have heard it. The echoes of their soles on the cobbles still reverberated, and their panting breath steamed in the air. A muffled cry was cut short behind the stone wall. A woman's voice.

Julian met Charlie's eyes for a split second, before the shorter man launched himself at the stone wall like a squirrel. Julian tried to follow. Charlie seemed to bounce up and scrabble over with a yell. Julian couldn't get a grip. He ducked back a couple of metres to the railing. The spikes scratched at the bottom of his coat as he leapt over the top. He could hear Charlie yelling. Julian hit the ground and looked up the path.

"Lizzie!" he cried as soon as he saw her.

Lizzie was collapsed back against the wall, clutching her throat as blood dripped between her fingers. Charlie was grappling with a tall man in black. Julian raced over. He threw his scarf around her, falling to his knees.

"Lizzie! Lizzie, look at me! Hold this on the wound, keep pressure on it! You're going to be okay!" He pulled the scarf around her, holding it to her throat to try and slow the bleeding.

Charlie had pulled them apart and punched her assailant in the face. The man staggered from the blow. He was shrouded in black, his face hidden by a deep hood, but the dark moustache was thick across his top lip. Charlie dove at him. The man lashed out with his knife. Charlie dodged and grabbed his wrist. He twisted the knife away, slashing the man across the forearm. The Jack yelped. His blood splattered the path. Charlie tried to throw the knife, but the Jack grabbed him again. They grappled over the blade. He was bigger than Charlie, but not as feral. He shoved the sleuth against the wall. Charlie kicked out. His foot caught the man's bag, knocking it to the ground. Glass shattered. The overpowering scent of formaldehyde filled the air.

The Jack slashed at Charlie again. Charlie hit the wall roughly, trying to dodge. The knife caught him across the ribs. He hissed, grabbing the Jack by the cut on his arm. The man yelled as Charlie twisted his wound. He grabbed Charlie by the hair and smashed the side of his head against the wall. Once. Twice. Charlie staggered. His ears rang and his vision blurred.

"Charlie!" Julian bellowed.

The Jack dropped him. Charlie fell to his knees. He pressed his hand to his ribs and felt blood coat his fingers. The Jack snatched his dripping bag from the ground. It rattled teasingly as he threw it over his shoulder and bolted. Charlie lurched, trying to give chase. His legs trembled and caved. Hands grabbed him.

"Oh, sweet baby Jesus, Sleuth, you've been stabbed," Julian muttered, holding him tightly.

"Not stabbed," Charlie mumbled. "Catch Jack…"

Julian was ignoring him, and the man was getting away. Charlie slumped in his friend's arms. His knees still quaked. He felt dizzy. Sick. His head hurt.

"I'm getting you and Lizzie home, Charlie," Julian assured. "Hold tight."

# 8

The night was dark and cold. It had begun to rain. Inside the room was toasty warm and embers still burned in the fire. Amy was snuggled down in her bed, fast asleep. She didn't wake when the door opened. She didn't wake when the dark figure crossed to her bed. It wasn't until the hand touched her shoulder and the voice whispered her name that she stirred. She groaned as she woke. The figure set a candle on her nightstand and lit her bedside lamp, throwing light across the room. Amy winced and grumbled.

"Harry…?" she muttered, struggling up. "What's going on?"

"I'm sorry to wake you…" he whispered. "I didn't know who else to come to."

She rubbed the grit from her eyes and then gasped in shock as she beheld the state of him.

"Oh my God! Harry! What happened?!" she exclaimed.

"I was mugged," he muttered. "Coming home from the club, someone attacked me, stole my wallet… ugh," he grunted, wincing as he perched on the side of her bed. "They could have just asked…"

"Let me see," Amy insisted, bundling her blankets

aside and crouching next to him to look. She hissed as she touched his face, turning his cheek towards the light. "That's certainly more than a scratch, my love."

"Amy…" Harry murmured, pressing his lips together nervously. "I… I'm sorry… about earlier… I– I never should've…"

"We both said some awful things," she agreed.

"I need you to know I didn't mean it," he begged, as she dug her medical bag out from under her bed. "I… I was talking with John at the club. I know I was a complete arse. I'm sorry, Amy, truly —"

She kissed his damp hair forgivingly.

"You think I haven't spent the rest of the evening wallowing in guilt under Daddy's reproving glower?" Amy smiled at him. "We're all childish sometimes, I'm just glad you're alive."

She reached out to take his hand, but it was clutching the bloody bandage on his arm.

"Oh God, Harry! How bad is it?" she demanded.

"This is the worst one," he admitted. "He… uh, he had a knife, but I took him on and he ran away. Think maybe I scared him."

"The bandage is filthy," she criticised, unwrapping the bloody slash on his arm. She could smell something chemical and sighed inwardly. Of course he'd tried to clean it himself. "I'm going to stitch you up, but then we have to call the police."

"That's not necessary…"

"It bloody well is," she retorted. "Hold still."

Harry grimaced painfully the entire time she cleaned and stitched the gash in his arm. He was deeply lucky the wound wasn't worse. It could easily have been a real problem. He looked like he'd knocked it, or worse. It was a mess, and he made such pitiful sounds as she patched him up.

"Oh Harry," she chuckled softly at one such whimper. She kissed his temple, avoiding the cut on his cheek. "You're doing great. I'll have you ready for the authorities in no time."

"I don't want to talk to them," he muttered. "Can't we… can't it wait until morning, at least?"

She sighed, tying off the stitches and snipping the thread.

"Please, Amy…" he begged. "I don't think I'm up for it tonight. We'd have to tell Dad, and I just… can't all of that wait until morning?"

"Very well," she relented. "When I'm done patching you up, I'll send you to bed."

"You're the best," he grinned, leaning in to kiss her.

"Hold that thought," she stopped him, a sudden chill settling in her blood as she took in the condition of his face.

"Amy?" he queried.

"Let me have a look at this," she replied softly, applying alcohol to a clean rag and dabbing at his cheek.

"How bad is it?" he asked, wincing again.

"It's not good…" she whispered. The chill had made it to her voice. She couldn't hide it. Her hands were shaking and she felt sick. She cleaned the cut carefully, almost scared to touch it on his swelled and bruised cheek.

"You're shivering," he commented, making her jump.

"It's okay," she assured weakly. "I'll have you ready to go in a second, then I can get back in bed."

"I could always stay..." he suggested, sliding his uninjured arm around her and pulling her close.

Amy shook her head violently, trying not to recoil.

"I don't think that's a good idea," she murmured nervously. "You've been injured. You need to rest."

"And you have graduation tomorrow," he sighed.

"Yes, yes of course," she agreed.

"Amy...?" He said her name so slowly she thought she might vomit. "What's wrong, Amy?"

"You mean aside from you showing up bloody and broken in my room in the middle of the night?" she retorted.

He pulled a face. Her comment was not unfair. But she knew that he knew that she knew something was wrong, and the thought made her want to scream. She could feel the fear building in her chest, crushing her lungs. She wanted to cry.

"Who did this to you?" she whispered.

"What do you mean?" he replied.

"Someone mugged you, Harry," she could feel herself choking on the lie. "Someone attacked you with a knife. What happened? Who was it?"

"Just... just some random man in the park," he answered. "I don't know. It was dark. I'm sorry I don't have more details."

"You didn't... there's no way you... you didn't go looking for any kind of fight, did you, Harry?"

"Of course not! Amy, why would you even ask that?"

"It's just…" her throat was so tight she could barely speak. "I guess, the city just feels like a very dangerous and violent place now… not even you can walk home safely…"

"Oh Amy," Harry sighed. He held her close and she wished she'd stop shaking, but she couldn't bring herself to hug him back. "I'm sorry," he apologised. "I didn't mean to scare you. I'll give a statement to the police in the morning, I promise. Although, I fear a statement won't be all that helpful. I didn't see much."

"No…" Amy whispered in sick dread. "No, I don't imagine you did…"

Charlie felt like he'd been hit in the head with a brick wall. Twice. Which he had. Which was probably why he felt like that. He touched the bump again.

"You doing okay, Sleuth?" Julian asked, his arm firmly around Charlie as they staggered down the street.

They had managed to get Lizzie safely back to the High House, whereupon the live-in doctors had descended upon them. Useful people, doctors, Charlie was finding. Lizzie was going to be okay, thank God. A second later and they might not have been so lucky. She was an idiot, and she knew it, but she had been caught by surprise and elbowed her attacker when they grabbed her. Then Charlie had dropped onto them from the sky — as she told it. They wouldn't let her talk much, but, fortunately, the wound to her neck was shallow. Unfortunately, she didn't get a better look at the man than they did.

The doctors had tended to Charlie's injuries, stitching up the gash across his ribs and warning him about his concussion. Julian had insisted on accompanying him home. Bronny wouldn't have let him leave if someone didn't take him.

"I've been worse," he sighed.

"You've been better too," Julian said. "That was insane, what you did tonight. If anything worse had happened to you, Bronny and Skipp would have had my balls."

"No one's going to hurt you on my account, Swift," Charlie grinned.

"Utter bull," Julian disagreed. "These people all love you, Charlie. I know you're too wrapped up in your own nonsense to notice, but they do. You're a rascal, but you're their rascal, and Heaven help anyone who threatens you."

"Aw, Swift…" Charlie cooed. "Do you say sweet things like that to Skipp as well?"

Julian glared at him. Charlie ignored the look and tenderly poked the welt on his head. There was still blood in his hair.

"Now I just need everyone to rally behind me to hunt that man in black," he muttered.

"You need a rest," Julian disagreed. "The cops came and took our statements. They'll get the guy. You need to take it easy."

"He was wearing all black…" Charlie continued to ignore Julian. "Robes or something under his coat. Like a priest… no. No… like… like a professor. And the formaldehyde! Now we know he's preserving the hearts! He's keeping them!"

"This doesn't sound like you resting, Charlie," Julian sighed.

"There is a mystery to solve, Swift!" Charlie protested. "Somewhere in this city is a tall man in black who is cutting out women's hearts and storing them in jars. Somewhere out there… and none of my investigations brought me to them. All that work… not a trace, all this time…"

"It's a mess, Sleuth, I won't deny you that." Julian walked him up the stairs and knocked on the front door. "But you need to rest that big brain of yours before it gets you killed."

It took a moment for someone to come to the door, and when it was opened Jasper stood there with his coat on over his nightclothes. He took one look at them and the colour drained from his face.

"Charlie!" he exclaimed, reaching for him. "What happened?!"

"He ran into the Jack of Hearts," Julian replied. "Our doctors patched him up. He's going to be okay. We just need to make him rest, which—"

"—Is not a task I would wish upon my worst enemy," Jasper commented drily. "In you come, Sir. The ladies have been dreadfully worried for you, as they so rightly should be."

"No, Swift," Charlie begged weakly. "Don't leave me with him."

"I said I'd get you home, Sleuth," Julian handed him over to the butler. "You'll be fine."

"No! Take me with you to see Skipp! I know things he needs to hear! We need to catch this man!"

"Goodnight, Charlie," Julian smiled.

"I won't interrupt! I can be good!" Charlie begged.

Julian shut the door in his face.

"Quickly Jasper!" Charlie patted the butler's shoulders urgently. "Upstairs!" He threw himself from Jasper's arms, staggered up the stairs, and crashed through his bedroom door.

Jasper followed wearily, heading further up to inform Susan and Rebecca what the cat had dragged in. Charlie collapsed on his window seat, clutching his ribs through his ripped and bloodied shirt. He peeked through the lace curtains and smirked as he watched Julian disappear around the back of the bakery.

It began to rain. It was a pity it hadn't started earlier. For one thing it could have helped to wash some of the blood away, and for another Charlie would have paid good money to watch Julian turn up on Michael's doorstep all bedraggled. But it did throw a spanner in the works of the case…

His fun was ruined by the arrival of his sisters. Rebecca stormed in and Susan followed sternly, both had their dressing gowns tied over their nightdresses. They did not look pleased.

"Charles Shilling!" Rebecca declared like he didn't know his own name.

Charlie rolled his eyes.

"What in God's name happened to you?" Susan demanded.

"I was bested by the Jack of Hearts," Charlie admitted. He stood and tried to draw himself up, but the wound pulled and his head spun. He nearly hit the ground. Rebecca caught him.

"You idiot," she scolded. "Let's get you properly cleaned up."

"Stop manhandling me!" he protested.

They ignored him and dragged him away from the window. Now, if there was any gossip to be spotted, he was going to miss it. Neither woman listened to a thing he said until they'd checked his bandages, changed his clothes, and washed the blood from his hair. Rebecca still treated him like he was a small child, but at least she knew better than to try and get the servants to clean him. Charlie was a strong, independent baby squirrel... and a feral biter.

"You could have gotten yourself killed!" Rebecca exclaimed for the dozenth time, as he wrested himself from her hands to button his own pyjamas.

"I could get killed crossing the road in the morning visiting the bakery!" Charlie protested. Rebecca pushed him down gently so that he was at least sitting on the edge of his bed, even if they couldn't get him to lie down. "Life is not without risk!"

"You know what she means, Charlie," Susan warned. "You were stabbed —"

"It's a mild cut," he argued. "At most, a very light stabbing. Trying to explain what happened to

139

Constables Wilson and Bond this evening was much more painful, I assure you. We're this close, Becky! This close! I've actually met the man, and I can track him. I know I can. I just have to get back there before the police bungle everything up or the rain destroys all trace of him! Everyone's making such a big deal over a wee scratch and a knock to the head—"

"We've been listening to you mutter since you got home, Charlie," Rebecca cautioned. "If your brains were anymore scrambled I could make an omelette from them."

"I'm not that bad!" he protested.

"You were talking about Amelia Florin's perfume," Susan reminded.

"It's relevant to the case!" Charlie cried. "Don't either of you listen?!"

There was a knock at the door. It boomed, deep and foreboding up the stairs in the otherwise quiet house. The rain was still lashing at the windows, drowning out other midnight noise.

"Swift...?" Charlie tried to stand, but Rebecca pushed him back down.

Footsteps sounded down the hall as Jasper went back to the door. Voices reverberated dimly as he answered. They heard his surprise, but not his words. Then someone was invited in. Jasper was leading them up the stairs. When he stopped in the doorway he looked more than a little surprised.

"Master Shilling, Lady Amelia Florin is here to see you," Jasper announced with a touch of uncertainty.

He stepped carefully aside as a rather sodden Amy

140

appeared in the doorway. Jasper had clearly already taken her cloak, but her skirts were so wet she looked like she'd walked here. Her dress had been thrown on hastily, and her auburn curls frizzed out the back of her bonnet like a halo.

"Florin…?" Charlie started slowly. "What are you doing out at night?! The Jack could've– ugh." He tried to stand, pulled his stitches, and doubled over with a grunt.

"You're hurt!" Florin started, stepping forward.

"I'm fine," Charlie replied, as Rebecca dumped him back on the bed.

"He's been stabbed," Susan announced sternly. "And concussed."

"I'm so sorry…" Amy whispered.

"You're soaking wet, darling, come stand by the fire," Susan insisted, taking charge of the situation. She swept forward, taking Amy by the shoulders and guiding her across the room to the space by the hearth, before turning back to Jasper. "Some tea, perhaps, Jasper?"

"Of course, my Lady. Right away," Jasper bowed and left the room.

"I'm so sorry to trouble you at this hour…" Amy muttered.

"Believe me, Miss Florin, we were already well troubled," Susan sighed.

Charlie was trying to worm out of Rebecca's grasp and flop across the bed to the other side of the room by the fire.

"Florin! Florin! You're never going to believe what

happened!" he cried. "I was wrong!"

"Yes, Charlie, we're all terribly shocked," Rebecca sighed.

"The Jack is the moustachioed man after all!" he declared, rolling painfully off the other side of the bed with a yelp and a thud.

"Charlie, get back in bed!" Becky hissed, hurrying around to grab him.

"He attacked us, Florin," Charlie straightened up awkwardly. "Poor Lizzie came down with a — hopefully fleeting — case of insanity. Some of the other women convinced her it was her fault what happened to Jenny, but she was smart enough to work out Jenny had gone to the White Swan on her own. So, overcome with madness, she decides she's going to get justice. Idiocy! But Swift and I managed to get to her in time — thank God."

"The Jack attacked her, not you…?" Amy asked, her voice trembling slightly.

"Her to start with," Charlie shrugged. "It's a miracle we got to her, but this wasn't like the previous attacks. He never engaged her services and she wasn't working. It was an ambush. She'll be okay, but he did manage to wound her before we got involved. I got a few good hits in before he took me down and ran off — turns out he's preserving the hearts! God only knows what for, but I broke a jar of formaldehyde in his bag, so I would guess the organs are being stored. It might help narrow things down. Talked to the police, for all the good that might do. Starting to drift away from a detective as a suspect though. Possibly an academic. The man was wearing black robes under his cloak, reminiscent of graduation gowns perhaps, or—"

"Barrister's robes," Amy interrupted.

"Yes!" Charlie pointed at her enthusiastically. "Yes, genius Florin! My brain is a little... concussed. Yes! Maybe even judicial..." he trailed off.

Amy had a hand pressed to her mouth as she failed to hold back a sob. Charlie paused mid rant to take in her condition. Amy turned her face away, trying to cover her distress with one hand and wave him off with the other. Susan took her by the shoulders comfortingly.

"Miss Florin...?" she murmured.

"I'm sorry..." Amy gasped, tears spilling down her face like a burst dam. "I'm sorry!"

"Are you all right, Miss Florin?" Rebecca asked.

Amy couldn't speak. She was trying to hold the sobs in, and failing. Her chest and shoulders trembled with the force of containing her distress.

Charlie muttered a rather obscene cuss.

"Charlie!" Rebecca exclaimed.

He ignored her. Charlie grimaced painfully, but didn't poke at any of his wounds again. He just watched the woman crying by the fireplace, his eyes full of pity.

"Florin, I am so, so sorry..." he muttered softly.

She cried harder. All his agitated exuberance had worn off. He stood strangely still and cocked his head to the side, the way he did when he was considering things.

"You're sure, aren't you?" he sighed. "You wouldn't be so upset if you weren't."

She gave up and buried her face in her hands. Susan

pulled a clean handkerchief from the pocket of her dressing gown, keeping an arm around Amy's trembling shoulders.

"I need you to run me through the evidence," he stated. "W-when you can," he added awkwardly, backing up to the edge of the bed and sitting down patiently.

Amy had taken the handkerchief, but she couldn't stop crying. Everyone else just waited. She could feel them waiting, but she couldn't breathe properly, let alone try and talk. Her breath was coming in small choking gasps, like she was having a panic attack. Maybe she was. Maybe the entire world was about to end, and she was the only one who knew, and she was falling apart.

But she wasn't the only one who knew. He knew. Shilling knew. She hadn't even had to say it. He'd worked it out, just by adding her tears to the pieces he had. Now he was sitting there, that way that he did, head cocked, like a well-trained puppy. Just waiting. Big eyes. Crooked lips pinched with pity. It just made it worse. His little scruffy puppy energy just made it all worse.

She wiped desperately at her face, trying to gulp one deep solid breath. She couldn't do it. She couldn't get enough air. Her eyes gazed around the room. She couldn't look at Shilling and his sisters. She couldn't meet their eyes. Shilling's room was as chaotic as his personality. Everything was shelves and stacks and piles. There were books strewn everywhere, like the man had robbed a library. The mantlepiece was home to a vast collection of small and beautiful pottery. The firelight gleamed off the patterns and glazes, lighting them from underneath.

Harry would die of rage if he knew she was here.

It was the first calming thought she'd had since she'd been woken. She took a deep breath, slowly steadying herself. Harry would be so angry he would froth at the mouth, and that was a very comforting thought. Amy gazed at the pottery on the mantle.

"These are very beautiful..." she said in a small voice, testing the strength of her words again.

"Thank you," Charlie replied. There wasn't the faintest trace of impatience. He was the calmest she'd ever seen him. "Which one's your favourite?"

"I think the red one..." she answered slowly. "With the roses. On the end."

"If you like it, you can have it," he offered.

"I'm not here to take anything from you, Shilling," she sighed deeply, drawing in a full and steady breath again as she turned back to him. "I'm here to tell you that Harry Pound is the Jack of Hearts."

"I'm sorry, who?!" Rebecca exclaimed.

There wasn't a shred of surprise in Shilling's face as he regarded her.

"That is an incredibly bold claim..." Susan stated, carefully trying to keep her tone even.

"It surely is," Shilling agreed, sitting calmly on his bed. "You're the only person who could make it, Florin, and even then it is still profoundly dangerous. To even breathe such a suggestion you would want to have irrefutable evidence behind you."

"I don't," she admitted, her voice shaking slightly and her fingers fidgeting with the tearstained handkerchief. "It... it doesn't even make any sense!" Her lungs trembled and she gave a dry sob. "He's squeamish! Everyone who knows him knows he's squeamish! It can't be him! But... but it is... that man you encountered in the park tonight... that was Harry."

"You're very sure about it," Shilling countered.

Amy took a deep, trembling breath. She could feel the tears starting to build again. Every time she had to think about it... about what she'd seen...

She took a deep breath in through her nose, and out through her mouth, and lifted her eyes to meet Shilling's gaze. His grey eyes were so calm. It didn't matter what she said now, he would believe her, no matter how far-fetched it sounded. He trusted her observation and he was happy to listen. It was a strangely humbling thought. No one had trusted her like that before. Not her father, not Harry, none of her professors. Shilling wasn't waiting to speak. He wanted to know what she thought. That was heartbreakingly rare.

"Is it awful..." she whispered, dropping her gaze again as she admitted what felt like a hideous sin, "that I had hoped he'd just started a fight with you, and that the Jack had nothing to do with it?"

Shilling gave a small laugh that turned into an abrupt 'ow'. When she looked up again he was touching his ribs.

"Harry was so angry tonight," she continued. "When I got home and told him what I'd been doing, he was disgustingly angry. I didn't understand. Then, when he came home injured, and I realised he'd been fighting with you… God, Shilling… so much of me hoped he was just a bigot, not a killer."

"But you knew better," Charlie replied, with his usual confidence.

Amy smiled. It seemed a weird time to be smiling, except she realised that the tone everyone else found so rude was probably one of the sincerest compliments she'd ever received.

"Nothing else made sense…" she confessed. "Not that this is much better."

"And therein lies the answer to the mystery," he spread his hands. "Finish the outline, cut away the shape, what do you have left?"

"The answer," Amy grimaced. "Harry went out to the Club tonight — he didn't specify which one, and he belongs to a few. It's a fairly standard occurrence. He has friends all over town. They drink and gamble… and generally behave like they're still college lads more often than they should. Debauchery isn't murder, but it means that any time in the past year Harry's stumbled home in a set of old shabby robes, we all assumed he was involved in silly drunken games or dares with the boys."

"The first thought was never 'my fiancé is a serial killer'?" Charlie quipped.

"It was not," Amy replied.

"What was different tonight?" he asked.

"He was injured," she answered. "He never comes to see me when he gets home. It was a first. He said he'd

147

been mugged, and I stitched up the cut on his arm."

She watched Charlie grimace when she mentioned it, just in case she'd had any doubts.

"I could smell the spilled formaldehyde, but I was hazy with sleep. At first I thought he'd just done something to try and clean the cut. Then I saw his face where you hit him." She pointed at Charlie's ring. "You've been fidgeting with that thing all day. I recognised the mark. That was when I knew he hadn't been mugged, he'd been fighting with you. Then…" her voice quivered again. She bit her tongue, trying to keep the tears from her voice. Goddamn, she didn't want to start crying again. Everyone was watching her so patiently. They weren't remotely judgemental. You probably didn't get a character like Charlie Shilling under your roof if there was a lot of judgement being passed. "There were traces of glue on his top lip," she stated clearly, listing things as impassively as she could. "His name was the top of the list you gave to Madam Bronny, but I was his alibi. After everything that was said about the victims today… I just… I don't know why he's doing it, but… it just… it can't be a coincidence. The robes, the bruise, the glue, the chemicals…"

Tears hit her like a steam train. She'd been doing so well, but she could feel them falling again. The handkerchief rushed back to her face and she buried her eyes in it, scrunching the soft fabric to her wet skin. She wanted to howl. Half of her understood logically the pieces all had to be put together, but half of her couldn't believe it was her Harry. He just wouldn't. He couldn't.

But he had, and now she was telling Shilling all about it.

"That's not enough to actively accuse him," Charlie sighed. "Certainly, between myself, Julian, and Lizzie, we would have some ground to stand on regarding the attack tonight, but you are the only witness to this other evidence which will all have been washed away by the morning."

He began to fidget with the buttons on the front of his pyjamas as he went into thinking mode.

"We need to find out what he's doing with the hearts…" Charlie muttered. "If we can find out why, or where, and catch him red-handed with the evidence… then we might stand a shot. It would be our only one though. Society is broken. You don't shoot for the son of the Lord Chief Justice and miss." He pulled a face and bounced up from the bed. The wound at his side tugged instantly and he staggered. All three women moved to catch him, but he grabbed the bedpost and steadied himself, waving them off.

"What are we going to do?" Amy asked in a small voice, knowing she wasn't going to like any of the answers, but unprepared for the sympathy of his actual reply.

"I'm going to find out what happened to Jasper and that tea, get you safe and comfortable, and then we're going to have to do some serious thinking," Charlie answered.

# 9

Dawn was beginning to break but the sky was mostly dark. The rain had stopped, yet the clouds were thick, and they were starting to turn pink. The room was lit by the fire, and it was warm and comfortable. Amy woke with a start on a bed that wasn't hers, slumped across a pile of pillows.

"Oh good, you're awake," Shilling commented from the window seat.

"I didn't mean to doze off…" she muttered, abruptly aware that she had somehow fallen asleep on his bed. With anyone else it would have been a scandal, but Shilling was as harmless as they came. The thought probably hadn't even occurred to him.

"You were exhausted and distraught. You needed the rest," he replied absentmindedly. "There's fresh tea on the table." He gestured vaguely at a pot and cups half hidden by books.

She kept her eyes on him. He was wearing his dressing gown backwards, snuggled up in it as he sat curled in the cushioned windowsill, staring out into the first break of day. He had his own mug of tea in one hand, and a pair of opera glasses in the other. Even as she watched, he peered out the window through the glasses with a small gasp, leaning forward.

"What? What is it?" she clambered from the bed and hurried over.

The street was softly bathed in pink and orange light. Not much seemed to be happening yet. She expected more traffic, but it was still early.

"Now, kiss!" Charlie demanded.

"Excuse me?" Amy looked at him, but he was ignoring her. He dropped the opera glasses with a disgusted groan.

"You useless twats!" he huffed furiously.

Amy looked out the window again as someone stepped out into the street from an alleyway she hadn't noticed before. The man straightened his dark coat against the cold dawn and tossed his curls imperiously. She recognised the heart-breaking handsomeness.

"Is that Julian Silver?" she asked.

"Yes," Charlie grumbled. "Useless twat."

"You want him to be kissing someone else?" She raised an eyebrow.

"I certainly don't want him kissing me," Charlie replied. "And I don't want him to, I *need* him to!" He keeled over gently and pathetically, tipping over his empty teacup. "You don't understand, Florin. They're my best friends and they're hopelessly in love and they're doing nothing to help themselves."

"I'm more familiar with the concept than you might think…" she sighed.

"At least your lesbian doctors aren't morons," he muttered from between cushions, catching on as fast as ever.

"Don't we have, uh... more pressing concerns?" Amy raised.

"Not really," Charlie sulked.

"Like the Jack of Hearts," she reminded coldly.

Charlie sighed and rolled himself from the window seat. He straightened up and tried to swing his robe the right way around. It ended with a yelp and a flinch.

"You know, the one who stabbed you," she added.

"I remember," he grimaced, touching the bandages. "The bulk of the case is solved now. We know who he is. That makes him significantly easier to thwart. Bringing him to justice may be profoundly difficult, but stopping him from hurting anyone else should be well within our means."

"This coming from the man who said he didn't want me returning home last night, because he thought it would be dangerous to put me back in a house with a killer targeting my look-alikes?" Amy snapped.

"Hm, yes," Charlie replied, casting his eyes down as he began to anxiously rub at a button. "Yes, I did say that..."

Amy took a deep breath and turned away, rubbing her temples. He was trying to be kind, God knew he was trying. He was trying in that terribly Shilling way. They both knew they couldn't just accuse Harry. That was a death sentence. Shilling wanted to keep her safe, and there was a part of her that was grateful. There was also a part of her that felt if Harry meant to kill her he would have done it by now. There was still a deep part of her, burning beneath the logic, that said it couldn't be Harry. It just couldn't. Maybe the incident last night tending to his wounds had all been a terrible nightmare and she'd overreacted. Maybe it was some bizarre coincidence that Harry and Shilling's injuries lined up. Because it couldn't be Harry. It could not.

But it was.

Amy felt like she was going to be sick. She took a deep breath, grateful that at least she wasn't crying again, and sat back on the edge of the bed once more. The painful fear and guilt gnawing at her gut made her wonder how she'd managed to fall asleep at all. Shilling was right though, she had been exhausted. Grief was like that.

Not for the first time, she perused the perilous stack of Dawson & Kropp books on his nightstand. It had made her chuckle at first. Somehow it was surprising Shilling collected erotic romance novellas. Now it felt like, after less than twenty-four hours in his company, she really shouldn't be surprised by anything anymore.

"I am concerned…" he murmured very slowly. There was a small sound of doubt. His hands had moved on from the buttons and he was now pacing slightly as he stimmed his loose dressing gown cord. "May I speak plainly, Florin?" he asked.

"I didn't know you knew how to speak any other way," she smiled, plucking the top book off the pile and flicking through the well-dogeared pages.

"Mm," he conceded nervously. "I am concerned for your safety. I do not wish to alarm or frighten you further, but many comments were made yesterday about your appearance in relation to the women the Jack has murdered. There is a connection. I cannot speak with exact certainty as to its nature, but current theories trouble me deeply."

"Why are all these little sections underlined?" Amy asked, ignoring his statement and noting repeatedly marked phrases and sentences. He didn't highlight a Dawson & Kropp book the way she would have, that was for sure.

"Oh, um…" He looked uncomfortable about being dragged off topic, but catered to her whim as best he could, a troubled crease forming over his brow. "That was just marking notes while I worked out who the Dawson & Kropp ghost writers were…"

"Of course you did…" she sighed. "For a case, I presume?"

"No…" Charlie shook his head. "Personal curiosity. Dawson & Kropp have twenty-six pen names but actually are only fifteen different writers, none of whom are called Dawson or Kropp. Of the fifteen, I am particularly fond of the work of three of them. So I worked out who they were so I could better follow their writing. I'm pen pals with one of them now. She's a grandmother in Southeast London who writes me delightfully erotic letters."

Amy laughed at him. She tried not to, shaking her head helplessly, but no matter how hard she pressed her lips together the giggles still escaped. It was all so terribly Shilling of him. Of course he had fan-stalked a grandmother to tell her how ardently he admired her erotic fiction. Eccentric was an understatement. She looked up at him and felt her smile slip as she met his eye. He was watching her with such earnest concern in his big eyes, head tilted, hair scruffy. His brows were sloped anxiously and his lips were pursed into a small frown. He was the complete opposite of everything she was used to.

"I'm glad you can laugh, Florin," he said softly. "But I do think it's important we have this conversation, when you're ready."

She sighed and stood, returning the book to the pile, and wandering over to admire the pottery again. If she was going to have to engage with the horror of reality, having something pretty to distract her eased the nausea.

"Do you really think Harry's going to kill me?" she asked, feeling her throat tighten. She reached up to run her finger along the floral pattern on the red vase.

"I honestly don't know," Charlie replied. "I think there is a very good chance that if he had realised last night what you knew, then you never would have made it here. That worries me, especially with regards to sending you back. We'll just have to be careful. I'll get my sisters to take you home. They can help cover for you. Then you just have to play it safe. Act naturally. Don't do anything stupid. After all, you have graduation to get through today."

"I can't think of anything less important than that right now," she sighed.

"Not at all, Florin," Shilling shook his head. "It is extremely important. Not just for your future, but to ensure you have one. Two days ago you would have cared. You need to care now. If Harry suspects you... I don't know what will happen, but I perish the thought."

"That's why we have to stop him," Amy countered. "I can't very well focus on anything else, Shilling. Harry — my Harry — is a killer! What am I supposed to do about that?!" She could hear the hysteria creeping back into her voice. The tears were building. Goddamnit.

"I'm working on some ideas," Charlie grimaced. "I... I feel perhaps you might truly be safer if you don't know. I don't want you dwelling on anything that might put you in harm's way."

"How gentlemanly of you," she snapped.

"Rather I think it's simply the responsible thing to do," he replied. "If you don't feel safe, Florin, say the word and we will put you up here. I will not make you go anywhere you don't want to. If you stay, he will almost certainly know and he will act accordingly. That will probably mean destroying evidence. I am more than prepared to risk that to ensure your safety, but ultimately the decision must be yours. Knowing what I know of you, I can't help but feel you probably don't approve of that idea, but you should know the option is there."

"You'd risk him realising we're onto him and destroying everything just to keep me away from him?" she echoed in astonishment.

"Of course," he shrugged. "We risk that even now. It's a perfectly acceptable risk."

"There are fifteen graves that would disagree with you," she said.

"That's a moot point," Charlie countered. "Those women are already dead, and the Jack only got close to Lizzie because she was mad with grief and decided to brave being the only woman out alone in London last night. That won't happen again."

"There are always vulnerable women," Amy reminded.

"But you don't have to be one of them," Charlie insisted. He was back to fidgeting with his ring. The same ring that had left the damning mark on Harry's cheek. Amy felt her heart sink further and further as she watched him. She knew what had to be done.

"I'm going to go home now," she stated softly, not quite prepared to admit the intensity of her reluctance.

"That is your decision to make," Charlie tipped his head respectfully. "I will let Susan know."

"What are you going to do about Harry?" Amy asked.

He was silent for a long moment, but she knew he was just thinking. He had his little thinking frown on. His head began to tilt slowly to the side. Her own smile widened as she watched the angle condense.

"Am I still invited to your graduation party tonight?" he asked.

"You are," she smiled.

"Then I will see you there, Doctor Florin, in the heart of the lion's den, as it were. Hopefully that will give us an opening to uncover irrefutable physical evidence and bring this entire nasty business to a close." He twisted his ring like he was trying to unscrew his finger. "Have you thought of something?"

"No." She shook her head, surprised he'd asked.

"Oh. Why are you smiling?" he inquired.

"I'm not," she replied automatically, the smile

vanishing. She felt it fall. That meant it had been there. She hadn't realised she'd been doing it.

"Okay," he nodded, turning to go.

She silently cursed herself. "Wait!"

He stopped and looked back from the doorway.

"I didn't mean to lie," she sighed. "I didn't realise I was doing it."

"I think that's normal behaviour," he replied. "We all do that sometimes. I'm glad you still have things to smile about. I'd be lying if I said I wasn't worried about you, Florin."

He turned to leave again. She didn't want him to go. She knew he had to get Lady Guinea and she had to go home, but she didn't want to. Not yet. Not quite. Not when his kind eyes felt like the only sane and normal thing left in the world.

"Charlie…" she called to him, causing him to pause again. He looked back at her in surprise. She froze. She had to say something. Now that she'd started she couldn't just leave it hanging. But… but what could she say? She certainly couldn't say everything she was thinking. Her own brain could barely wrap itself around her thoughts right now, and any concept of articulating her feelings just sounded inappropriate. Finally, she manged to settle on two words, and just had to hope they conveyed enough. "Thank you."

He gave her a polite nod.

"Of course, Florin," he replied. "You're most welcome." There was an empathy in his tone that made her feel weak, like he really did understand, but her efforts ultimately failed her. He turned and left the room, striding away up the stairs. She was painfully sorry to see him go.

The street was bustling and the noise of people and traffic had risen to a din. The sky was overcast with the heavy threat of drizzle, but the air didn't smell damp yet. It was too busy smelling of bread. Charlie just wanted to lie in his cushioned nook with the window open and breathe deeply. Rebecca wholeheartedly supported that plan to rest his injuries, and he wished he could do her proud. Unfortunately, the world called.

Susan had taken Florin home, which meant that once Charlie was dressed it was time for an appointment at the bakery. The crowd inside was dense and the queue long, so he dodged around the back and banged on the door usually reserved for Michael's runners. Charlie was not technically a runner, but sometimes he was as good as and Michael always let it slide.

"The man of the hour," he addressed Charlie with a cheeky grin as he opened the door.

"Whatever Swift told you, I'm sure he exaggerated," Charlie replied.

"It's not him you have to worry about, Sleuth," Mike said, tapping him on the chest with a folded newspaper.

Charlie took the paper and opened it up. Giant block letters on the front spelled out 'JACK THWARTED'.

"Bronny's let her people talk to the papers," Michael added. "Here was I foolishly thinking I was ahead of the game, and everything I bought from Swift showed up on my doorstep this morning. You're lucky they've never gotten a photo of you, Charlie. You'd be as famous as the Queen this morning."

"Charles Shilling bravely took on the Jack and saved the young woman's life… the notorious detective was heroically injured but is confident he will get his man…" Charlie read aloud slowly. "Witnesses can attest that the killer is a tall man with a dark moustache dressed in black robes. Please notify police if you have seen anyone fitting that description around the nights of the killings…" He scrunched the paper back into a roll. "Who wrote this tripe?! Witnesses? What bloody witnesses and why didn't they give us a hand? A few more people and he wouldn't have gotten away!"

"Good to see you up and about this morning though," Mike eyeballed him. "The way Swift told it I was a bit worried about you."

Charlie glowered and bonked him on the head with the paper.

"I saw you this morning. You didn't even kiss him goodbye!" he rebuked.

"He works for me, Charlie. There are moral dilemmas with kissing people who work for you — ow!"

Charlie hit him on the head again.

"If you do that again I'm not giving you any bread!" Mike warned.

Charlie smacked him repeatedly with the newspaper.

"This is more important than bread!" he declared.

"You don't mean that!" Michael gently fought him off and wrestled the paper away. "I know you, Charlie. You do not mean that."

Charlie stood small and forlorn in the doorway.

"You're different around him, Skipp," he insisted sadly. "You spend longer meeting with him than any of your other runners — than most of them combined. You hold yourself different around him. You smile more—"

"Charlie—" Mike protested. He gave a frustrated scoff, pulled a wrapped butter knot from his apron pocket, and shoved it in Charlie's mouth. "Just shut up, Sleuth," he blushed. "I don't need you doing your weird analysis on me."

Charlie took a bite out of the soft crusty bread and spoke around it.

"He likes you too. You should say something."

Michael flicked open the paper and eyed the headline again, seemingly ignoring Charlie, who took the opportunity to shove more bread in his mouth.

"You're lucky you earnt that last night, or I wouldn't be feeding you," Michael grumbled. "But you need your strength to catch the man who attacked you, before he hurts someone else."

"I'm not sure strength is what I'm going to need," Charlie muttered. "I need wiles and a complete disestablishment of the class system to get this psychotic killer…"

Michael folded up the paper with a sharp look at Charlie. Charlie met the look with big puppy-dog eyes, tearing and eating more bread.

"You know who he is," Mike accused.

"I do," Charlie admitted.

"Swift didn't say…"

"He doesn't know," Charlie replied. "He doesn't know who the Jack is and he doesn't know that I do know. Don't worry, Mike, he didn't hide anything from you. He wouldn't do that."

"But you hid it from him?" Michael deduced.

"Something like that," Charlie finished his bread. "This is dangerous, Skipp. It's more dangerous than we realised. We're not just dealing with a crazed killer. This is someone who…" Charlie trailed off. His crooked mouth scrunched in thought for a moment, and then he smiled a very bleak and tortured smile. "This is someone much, much smarter than I ever gave them credit for. I know it's hard to believe, but it's a lot safer for people not to know what I do. Anyone who learns the truth is in trouble… and…" he paused again, "and there's someone in particular I am worried for." He stopped somewhat abruptly and dusted his fingers on his coat. "Do you have any work for me?"

"You're in the middle of trying to catch the Jack of Hearts," Mike pointed out, clearly aware that Charlie was avoiding a specific topic of conversation.

"I have that in hand," Charlie shrugged. "I know who he is. I know how to protect people from him. Perhaps working on something else for a while will help turn my brain around and get the ideas flowing."

Michael reached back into the pocket slowly and withdrew a small, dusty, folded piece of paper. Charlie reached for it, but Mike pulled it back at the last second.

"Who are you worried about?" he asked. "It's not

like you to get so personal."

"It's safer if no one knows," Charlie replied, reaching for the note again.

"Okay, but," Mike pulled it out of reach again, "as your friend, Charlie, what are you getting mixed up in, and what does it have to do with Doctor Florin spending the night in your room?"

Charlie looked like he was about to bite. Mike knew the face. He grinned.

"Don't," Charlie warned.

"It's annoying, isn't it?" Mike pressed.

Charlie snatched the paper, wincing and grabbing the bandages under his shirt as he pulled his wound.

"She is in danger because she knows too much, Skipp," he grunted painfully. "Don't make the same mistake."

"Gossip is my business, Charlie," Mike warned.

"And I'm grateful you share it," Charlie replied. "But I already have one friend to worry about, Mike. Please don't try for two."

"Friends already?" Michael grinned. "Usually takes you longer than that."

Charlie shrugged. He didn't have a firm grasp of the situation as it stood, being that he was caught in the centre of it. It would take time to work out exactly how the chips would fall. Yet, he was fond of the doctor. She was kind and brilliant and… well… striking, in her own way. She had called him Charlie this morning. He hadn't realised they were on a first name basis yet, and hadn't known how to react. She'd been so frightened, so he'd kept it simple, but she'd called him Charlie like his friends did. Now, he had a painful need to keep her from harm, and the dreadful knowledge that such a thing was impossible. He was going to have to go after Harry Pound, and whichever way that went, one of them was going to end up swinging. Amy wouldn't be happy with either outcome. Charlie was going to have to settle for making sure she came out of it alive.

"I'm going to sort these this afternoon and work out how to catch the Jack," he announced, holding up the folded list. "Your job is to talk to Julian."

"It is, and I do it most days," Mike replied drily.

"You know what I mean, Skipp," Charlie sighed. "Tell him how you feel. He'll reciprocate."

"I can't afford him," Michael muttered. "And I don't want to share him."

Charlie stared at him, but Michael wouldn't meet his eye. A scarlet blush had stained his cheeks, bleeding through his pained expression. He reached into his apron pocket again, and pulled out another knot, slapping it into Charlie's hand.

"Stay out of my business, Sleuth, and I'll stay out of yours."

Charlie weighed up the bread in one hand and the note in the other. He smiled and bopped Michael on the nose with the knot, leaving an extra smear of flour dusted on his friend's face.

"No," he grinned, and bit off a large chunk of bread before declaring in a muffled tone, "I want you to be happy."

Michael looked torn between hugging him and hitting him. Charlie chose for him, catching him with one arm and squeezing him while being careful of his injury. Before Mike could change his mind, Charlie gave him an affectionate kitten-like bunt with his head, shoved the bread in his own mouth, and scampered away.

# 10

The carriage rolled up outside the wrought iron gate. Amy stared through the window at the front door. She definitely felt like she was going to be sick. Susan Guinea sat across from her, prim and proper as ever. She had tried to hold polite, and probably distracting, conversation with Amy when they had set off, but Amy just didn't have the will for it. She felt awful, like she was caught in the middle of a hurricane, and she couldn't breathe properly, and it was almost certainly going to kill her, but it hadn't yet, so she had all this time to contemplate her impending demise. She didn't like the way Lady Guinea was smiling at her. This did not feel like a smiling matter.

"Pull yourself together, Miss Florin," Susan ordered as the carriage stopped.

"Yes, Lady Guinea," Florin nodded meekly.

The door opened and the footman appeared. Susan looked like she was about to rise when she saw the man's face.

"What is it?" she asked.

"Thought perhaps you would like to know, before you go inside, my Lady, that Charlie is on the front page of the paper again," he warned her politely. "Just in case anyone asks."

"Do they have a photo of him yet?" she inquired.

"They do not," the footman smiled.

Susan smiled back. "Goodness, that boy gets around. Thank you for letting me know."

"Of course," he bowed, and helped her from the carriage.

"What does it say?" Amy asked nervously, following her out.

The footman handed her a copy of the paper. She unfolded it, her heart sinking down into the empty depths of her stomach. Reading about the event as told by someone else gave it an all new horror. They were ruined. Everyone in the city knew Charlie had tangled with the Jack now. They were going to be expecting an arrest any minute... and what they were going to get...

Oh God, if Charlie came for Harry without real evidence they were going to get a bloodbath, but short of catching him in the act, what were they supposed to do? Short of triggering Harry into going after her, what was their best plan?

Amy kept her nose buried in the paper as she followed Lady Guinea to the door. This wasn't something she was looking forward to anyway. It was nice to have a shield, even a paper one, and she wasn't wrong to be concerned.

When they got inside, it was very clear that the Pounds had been losing their minds at finding her gone. Henry in particular had woken to find his son injured and his daughter missing, and he descended on her in an even mix of embrace and scolding. The tighter he squeezed her, the harsher his lecturing became.

"Daddy, have you seen this?!" Amy demanded, worming from his arms and waving the paper.

Henry stared at her with an intensity that tried to convey how much trouble she was in despite their present guest.

"I am truly sorry, Lord Pound," Lady Guinea apologised again.

"Please, my good Lady, you have nothing to be sorry for," Henry waved her off.

"Consider my apology on behalf of my brother-in-law," Susan sighed. She gave Amy a look. "The children may be shockingly intelligent, but it would seem they are not always wise."

"Indeed," Harry agreed cuttingly from the corner of the room. The bruise on his cheek shone like a star and only made his anger look crueller. "I thought I was bad, but the recklessness you have shown, Amy—"

"My recklessness?!" she yelled at him, barely able to contain what she knew.

"Yes, your recklessness!" he bellowed. "Yes, your impudence! With everything going on, you thought you could just run off alone in the middle of the night?!"

"Good Heavens, no," Susan shook her head, stepping between them as Henry tried to wave them both down. "Miss Florin might be a fiercely independent young lady, but she's not stupid, Pound. She didn't go anywhere alone — a tactic that might have benefited you. An associate of my brother let her know what had happened."

"No one mentioned seeing anyone," Henry

frowned.

"Julian has a way about him," Susan stuck unflinchingly to her lie. "You have to meet the man to understand, but I have heard he is very hard to say no to, and that he is very good at showing up in ladies' room after hours."

"Lady Guinea!" Amy exclaimed.

"Not that I would ever imply such a thing about you, my dear," Susan smiled.

"And Shilling sent a man like that to — what? To bring Amy to him?" Harry blustered.

"Julian is a gentleman, and so is Shilling," Amy snapped. She needed the anger to keep away the tears. She was also slightly miffed that Julian hadn't actually shown up outside her window last night but leant into the lie. "How dare you? All of you. Shilling and his friends were attacked by the Jack of Hearts last night! They could have been killed! This is not the time to be condemning my relief efforts."

"It is if you're putting yourself in danger, love," Henry disagreed, looking between his children. "All these assaults and injuries last night... did no one consider going to an actual hospital?"

"Apparently not," Susan smiled. "Between our boys, Henry, young Florin here will be able to open her own clinic when they give her the certificate this afternoon."

"I hardly think she'll be interested in such an endeavour, Lady Guinea," Harry sniped. "If we can even get her to attend her graduation, instead of running off with your feral brother..."

"Harry," Lord Pound warned.

Amy stared across the room at Harry. She glared. There was so much she wanted to say. There was so much she wanted to attack him with before she tied him to the balcony and helped the police raid his room. But she couldn't do that, as logical as it felt, because no one would take her word over his. The notion that Harry Pound was the Jack? Preposterous. A gentleman would never. Shilling knew better, and Amy wished he was here right now. Her breath was catching again, the fear was building as she tried to hold Harry's eye. She missed Charlie.

"I saw his wounds…" she said softly, thinking about the strange little detective and how safe he felt. It was enough to provoke the homicidal twitch Harry couldn't hide whenever she expressed familiarity with Shilling. She couldn't believe she'd never noticed that before, and wondered if he'd been triggered by others in the past before she'd realised. She drove her point harder. "I saw how he was injured. You're lucky, Harry. It's possible you two were attacked by the same man…"

Silence settled as she tried to outstare him. He didn't flinch. There was a discomfort in his eyes, a distrust, but he wasn't going to break. Not before she did. The pressure in her chest was making it hard to breathe. She couldn't stay here.

"I have to go and get ready for the ceremony, but you should consider aiding us later, Harry," Amy suggested as she headed from the room. "You might find you know something that will help us catch the Jack."

She didn't wait for a response. She couldn't withstand his scrutiny any longer. He might be able to hide an entire double life as a serial killer, but Amy couldn't maintain the lie. She couldn't keep meeting his eye and pretending she didn't know. She curtsied to the other two as she headed from the room.

"Lady Guinea, thank you for looking after me and bringing me safely home. Daddy, I'm sorry I scared you. I didn't realise I would be gone so long. I promise I won't do it again."

They gave her gracious nods and didn't hold her up. She left the room with poise and grace, but stumbled on the stairs. One hand caught the rail, the other still clutched the rolled-up paper. She was so tired. The thought of trying to survive the day was unbearable, but hopefully a bath and change of clothes would help.

She was hugging the paper to her chest now, not even sure why. The ink was starting to smudge across her fingers. Harry's dig hurt. Not as much as reality. Her biggest problem was that she still didn't know how she felt. Scared, horrified — obviously. Heartbroken. Confused. Confusion felt like a fairly dominant emotion right now. Still, it wasn't going to stop her from putting one foot in front of the other. She could get up the stairs, then, if she really wanted to, she could sit in the bath and cry for a while.

Or so she thought. As she moved down the hallway a creeping dread stopped her. Harry's room. His bedroom door was closed, darkening the hallway. If there was any evidence to be found, surely it would be in there. If there was anyone who was going to find it, surely it was her.

She crept up to the door and turned the handle. The

drapes were wide open and the bed was neatly made. Everything was clean and tidy and organised. It did not look like the room of a crazed killer. Besides, where would he keep things that the servants wouldn't find? Fifteen human hearts in preserving jars were no small stash, and that was presuming there weren't other previous trophies from victims no one knew about yet.

That thought brought the nausea back. Amy retched weakly, pushing the sickness down. She could do this. She dropped the paper on the bed and crouched down, checking underneath. Nothing. She didn't know what she'd been expecting. Maybe a box of human remains. That was silly. As she stood again, she glimpsed herself in his bedroom mirror. She froze.

The daylight was soft and pale. So was she. She looked crazy. Her hair was frizzing out the back of the bonnet she hadn't removed when she came inside. There were shadows under her eyes that made her skin look washed out and sickly. Her clothes were scruffy and mismatched, just as she had haphazardly dressed herself, half in her night things, last night before sneaking out.

This was insane. There was no solid evidence against Harry. It couldn't be him. There were so many reasons it couldn't be him. In the clear light of day, without the stress of night and blood and fear, there was simply no way it could be Harry. She'd been mad at him for behaving so badly over Shilling, and now she was seeing things that weren't there. Harry had been mugged. It was a coincidence. She had to send Shilling a note to let him know she had been wrong, and then she had to get to her graduation and stop pretending to be a detective.

"Amy?"

She whirled around. Harry was standing in the doorway. His brown eyes were hard, but concerned.

"What are you doing in here?"

"I... uh..." she stammered. She hadn't heard him sneak up on her. "I'm not sure... um... the- the paper!" She glanced it on the bed. "I was dropping it off for you... uh..."

Harry crossed the room, closing the gap between them as she spoke. Her words stuttered and cut off weakly. She couldn't tell him the truth. He reached her, placing his hands either side of her shoulders and staring down at her.

"Are you all right?" he asked. "You don't look well, Amy."

"I know..." she grimaced. "I look a right mess, don't I?"

"It's concerning, to say the least," he admitted. "You... you know you can tell me what's wrong, Amy — whatever it is — I'm sure we... we can..."

"I promise you, Harry, if I could articulate the problem, I would have done it by now," she sighed, leaning into his embrace.

He slid his arms around her shoulders, pulling her in and holding her tightly. She slipped her arms around his waist and buried her face in his collar. He was so warm and familiar. He smelled like home. There was no way he could be a killer, and she felt like an idiot for even thinking it. Maybe, once Shilling caught the real

Jack, she could tell Harry what she'd thought and they'd laugh about it — about how foolish she'd been.

"You keep changing the rules on me," Harry muttered. "I thought we were good again, after you helped me last night, but then you were gone this morning… I don't know what to do about you, Amy, I really don't."

She swallowed nervously. How foolish she'd been…

Charlie didn't think she was foolish. He had believed her. He had trusted her medical opinion and asked for her help. Her medical opinion was certain that Harry had been the one Charlie fought with last night. Their injuries lined up perfectly. Doctor Florin knew that, but Amelia Florin couldn't lose Harry Pound. Harry's grip on her tightened.

"There's nothing I wouldn't do for you, Amy," he whispered. "Nothing. I need you to know that. I need you to understand."

"I do," she gasped, trying to head him off. She needed him to stop speaking. Yesterday it would have felt romantic. Now it felt threatening. His arms around her were no longer sure and comforting. They trapped her. Bound her. Her heart was racing. There were two conflicting truths fighting for dominance in her mind.

It wasn't possible that Harry could have hid something like this from her their whole lives. She would have known. She would have seen. Maybe she had. Maybe there had been little moments. Besides, what was the alternative? Shilling could be lying. She didn't really know him.

That wasn't true. She didn't have to know him.

Charlie wore his heart on his sleeve. He had been stabbed last night trying to save a woman from a man in black… this man. Amy remembered Lizzie from the High House, the poor grief-stricken lady who had been so distraught over her friend's death. Over Jenny's death.

The memory of the morgue flared with a dizzying wave of nausea. Harry still held her. His hands on her body… these hands… these were almost certainly the hands that had murdered Jenny. It made no sense, but it was the only thing that made sense. She wanted to scream. She needed to scream. She needed to know why…

"Tell me what's going on…" Harry breathed against her ear. "What do you need from me, Amelia? Say the word."

She ripped herself from his arms, spinning towards the bed and snatching the paper as she steadied herself. She thrust the newspaper at his chest.

"Look at it," she ordered. "Help us catch the Jack."

"Amy…" Harry sighed wearily.

"Do it," she insisted, smacking the paper against his shirt hard enough that he raised his hands to take it from her. "Shilling will be here tonight. Talk to him. Compare wounds, Harry." She stared him down so hard the fear nearly left her. She could feel her lungs heaving as she breathed deeply, confidently. She stared him straight in the eye. "Do the right thing. That's what you can do for me."

She didn't know if it would work. It seemed like a long shot, but it was the best one she had. He said there was nothing he wouldn't do for her, hopefully that included coming clean about everything — whatever everything turned out to be. If he was innocent, the evidence would prove it. If he wasn't...

If he wasn't, then she had to know. She had to know for sure.

She left him with the newspaper and strode from the room. She couldn't solve the case alone. If she could get Harry to agree to help Charlie, then they would get their answers. One way or another.

# 11

The clouds had burnt off and the day was proving fine. Amy wished she could say the same about herself. She was doing much better than she had been that morning, but she was starting to wonder if perhaps she would never be fine again. At least she had managed to convince herself that none of it was her problem for the next few hours.

She was dressed and robed up. Her curls were carefully smoothed and pinned beneath her cap. A stage and vast rows of seats had been erected out on the university lawn. It was a beautiful day for it. She wished she could get in the mood, but death still hung over her like a cloud. She was the only one who couldn't behave normally. The Pounds were with her, happily hobnobbing with other graduates and their friends and family. Amy found she could barely smile.

"You don't have to be nervous, love," Henry whispered, appearing at her side and slipping a supportive arm around her shoulders.

"I know, Daddy. I'm sorry," she sighed.

"You don't have to be sorry either," he chuckled and kissed her cheek. He paused a moment, holding close. Amy couldn't take her eyes off Harry as he shook hands with the endless crowd of admirers and sycophants. The future Lord Pound had always been very popular. Amy couldn't wrap her head around the notion that he might kill someone. The evidence that he had attacked Lizzie was so strong, but the motive was completely lacking. Why on earth would he do such a thing?

Henry moved into her line of sight, blocking her view as he took her hands and tried to face her.

"Amy, darling, you'll tell me, won't you?" he asked softly. "When you feel up to it, you'll tell me what's wrong? You know you can tell me anything."

A horrible lump blocked her throat and her eyes began to water. She wished that were true. It should be true. But it wasn't. This was probably the only thing in the world she couldn't tell him. She'd never wanted to be wrong about anything so badly in her life. She nodded meekly, hoping that would be enough.

"Okay," Henry sighed, hugging her gently and kissing her cheek again. There was a loving and resigned acceptance to his tone — like he knew he couldn't get more from her yet, but he also knew to be patient.

Someone came by calling all the graduates to fall in, and a mass of black robes began to drift away from their supporters to congregate elsewhere while everyone found their seats. Henry patted her shoulder supportively as they moved to part.

"Daddy, wait—" Amy turned to him sharply.

"What's wrong?" he asked.

"You… do you… you trust Charles Shilling, don't you?" she pressed. "That's why you let him work with the police, even though he's technically unqualified, and why you let him get away with all the bizarre things he does?"

"What's he done, Amy?" Henry demanded quietly.

"Nothing!" she shook her head. Dear God, she had no idea how to broach her fears on this with him. Henry watched her shrewdly. Amy felt her heart blocking her throat. Henry stopped her a moment longer, deep understanding in his eyes.

"You know... knowledge is never wasted, my love," Henry encouraged softly.

Amy looked at him in confusion. Henry gazed at her supportively.

"If... if this is personal, darling," he spoke gently. "If Shilling did that thing he does... if he told you that he knows you don't really want to be a doctor because of the way you tie your shoes or something —"

Amy covered her mouth as she laughed. Henry smiled.

"If that is what is going on," he pressed, "it's all right. You got this qualification because you wanted to be a doctor. If you don't want that anymore, no one would blame you, but you earnt the knowledge, you deserve to graduate, and what you learnt will never be wasted regardless of whether or not you choose to practice."

"Thank you, Daddy," Amy squeezed his hands gratefully. "It's nothing like that though. I'm not scared to graduate... I... I just... I'm scared of life, I think..." she didn't know how to say it.

"Life is a big and scary thing," Henry agreed. "I am

struggling a little to connect your graduation anxiety to
Mister Shilling, however. Are you sure he didn't say
something inappropriate?"

"I'm sure," Amy smiled weakly. "He's actually been
very complimentary about my skills. As far as I'm
aware, I think he thinks I'd make a good doctor. This
isn't about that. I… I just want to trust him. With
everything going on at the moment… I need to be able
to trust him, but I barely know the man. It helps to think
that you trust him too. I know opinions on him are
divisive…"

"You mean the papers think he's a hero, provided
they don't have to interact with him, and Harry hates
him with the ferocity of a spoilt child?" Henry raised a
giant bushy eyebrow.

Amy pinched her lips together. Henry smiled.

"I know my son, darling," he continued. "Don't let
Harry's rumours scare you. To answer your initial
question, yes, Amy, I trust Shilling. I've always found
the boy's heart to be in the right place, even if his head
is up in the clouds or digging through a closet."

"You do know them well… don't you?" Amy
mused, realising that perhaps it was Henry who she
should have come to all along. "Daddy, have you
noticed anything odd about Harry or Charlie recently?"

"Oh Amy…" Henry chuckled. "Don't let the boys
and their tiff trouble you. I promise you, their issues are
not as nefarious as they might seem. Harry's a good
boy, but if he has one sin it's his jealousy. When Shilling
first showed up and took down Kopeck, Harry was in
law school and he was spitting at the vigilante

investigating of it all. He wasn't wholly wrong, some of Shilling's methods are dubious, but the boy gets results and he never hurts anyone to get them. Harry never liked that I took a shine to the lad, and he's getting quite worked up over the notion that you might have time for him too. Let him behave like a child for now, hold your ground, and when he calms down he'll realise he's made an arse of himself. A little bit of humility will be good for him, I think."

"You think they're fighting over me?" she sighed.

"I don't think Shilling knows how to fight over a woman, darling," Henry chuckled. "He knows Harry doesn't like him, and he's nobody's fool. I wouldn't worry about it — but tell me if it's making you uncomfortable. If I have to lay down the law with Harry, I will. He's been a right brat the last few days."

"That he has…" Amy agreed sickly, realising that Harry had been excessively arrogant this week even before Shilling was dragged into their dining room.

"I'll talk to him," Henry assured. "Is that all that's troubling you? You're worried about trusting Shilling, he didn't say or do anything?"

"No," Amy sighed. "No, Shilling isn't what troubles me. He's a harmless wee thing. Quite sweet, really. Don't tell Harry I said that."

"I won't," Henry smiled. He patted her shoulder. "Shilling's a good man, Amy. You can trust him. He'll get the Jack. Now, go join your friends and don't worry about it so much." He urged her forward and she hurried away to catch up with the other graduates, keeping the crowd between her and Harry. Part of her knew he would be looking to wish her luck, and she couldn't stomach another conversation with him right now. Every single one felt like a test, like she was walking a tightrope and might stumble and fall any second, revealing a deadly revelation.

She delicately hoisted the front of her gown and hurried to join Laura and Jane. They grinned and waved her over as she fell in with them.

"What was all that about?" Jane asked quietly.

"Dad was just wishing me luck," she replied breathlessly. "And telling me not to worry."

"I meant what was with the cold shoulder you just gave Harry…" Jane clarified.

"Are you two still fighting after yesterday?" Laura asked.

"He's not exactly been well-behaved recently," Amy muttered.

"You weren't the one who did that to his face, were you?" Jane checked.

"I was not…" Amy breathed, aware that her tone wasn't convincing, but unable to muster anything better. Now didn't seem like the right time to tell them she was fairly certain who had done it. Maybe she could get their opinions on the injury later. Maybe they would disagree with her conclusion and it would turn out Harry really was mugged after all. A huge misunderstanding…

She didn't know how many times she could keep fooling herself by repeating that theory. It was starting to run dry. She was bouncing between denial and anger like she had springs glued to her feet. Worst of all… she wished Charlie was here. She was barely holding in a meltdown, but having him around, just *knowing*... knowing in that way he did, and her knowing she wasn't alone, it would help. Still, she just had to get through the ceremony.

They were carefully ordered and seated. Amy barely paid any attention to the speeches. She barely paid attention to any of it. If Laura and Jane hadn't been there to guide her, she was worried she would have missed all her cues. Fortunately, they dragged her with them to the line by the stage. There was an eruption of polite applause as her name was called and she crossed to the podium. She shook the Chancellor's hand and took her scroll, glancing at the crowd. It was impossible to make out her family in the ocean of faces. But something did stand out.

A large tree rose tall and slender beyond the lawn, its dark woody branches grasping helplessly at the sky. Someone stood in front of it, someone slight in a long tan coat, looking small and pale against the rough bark. She barely glimpsed him before she had to keep walking, nearly stumbling down the stairs at the other end. Without the vantage of the stage, the bottom of the tree was lost behind the crowd. She couldn't spot him again. Had something happened? Did he need her help?

She was ushered into line with the others as they were slowly filed back to their seats. Jane touched her arm gently.

"Are you all right?" she whispered.

"I think I just saw Charlie," Amy blurted.

There was a raised eyebrow. Amy wasn't sure if it was because she'd used his first name, if it was because Jane thought she was hallucinating, or if it was just because she had that startled bunny energy again. She could barely contain herself as she was forced to sit through the rest of the ceremony. She turned to look twice, but she couldn't see the base of the tree from down here, and the look Jane directed at her was sharp enough to caution her curiosity.

He was gone when she finally got free. If he'd even been there at all. Maybe she really was seeing things. Maybe it hadn't been him. Her heart sank as she watched the lone tree. Arms grabbed her from behind. Her startled yelp was drowned out by a laugh in her ear.

"I didn't mean to scare you," Harry chuckled, holding her close.

Amy pressed her lips together, hiding her grimace. Her heart was racing more than it should have been. Foolish. Everything she did now felt foolish. Everything since dashing from the house in the middle of the night. Since running to see Charlie.

"What are you looking at?" Harry asked, his cheek pressed to hers as he followed her line of sight to the tree.

"Nothing..." she answered weakly.

"It's a nice view," Jane commented pleasantly, coming up beside them.

Harry's arms slipped from around her and he bowed politely at the ladies.

"Congratulations, M.D.s," he grinned.

"Thank you, Harry," Laura curtsied coyly at him. She bounced towards Amy and clutched her shoulders. "I'm sure Amy would be more than happy to *thoroughly* check you over, should you require it…"

"Laura!" Amy exclaimed as her friend giggled cheekily at her.

"Too soon, Doctor Mark," Harry smiled. "I appreciate your insinuations, but I did actually require Doctor Florin's medical assistance last night." He took Amy's hand and kissed it gratefully.

"I heard someone say you got mugged?" Jane inquired carefully.

"Mm," Harry touched the large, dark bruise on his cheek. "Other man had it worse though," he bragged. "Didn't know who he was messing with."

That was certainly true, Amy thought to herself. At the time Charlie hadn't known who he'd been up against, save that it was a man bigger and stronger than him, and he'd ended up stabbed. Lightly stabbed, as he liked to put it.

"Yes, it was a dangerous night to be out last night," she said pointedly.

"And yet…" Harry tried to insinuate darkly.

"And yet you were," she retorted. "But that's all right, we're going to put a stop to the attacks."

"You never did tell us how your investigation went yesterday," Laura piped up.

"It was as illuminating as it was horrifying," Amy replied. "I've invited Charlie to come to the party tonight and let us know what he's found today. I also want to have him and Harry compare injuries. I believe they were attacked by the same man."

"No!" Laura gasped. She clutched Harry's shoulder. "You were attacked by the Jack?!"

"I think not…" Harry grimaced. "Really, Amy, it was just a mugging. I do worry, darling, that all this Jack business is going to your head."

"It can't hurt to talk to the man, Harry," Jane commented softly. Everyone fell quiet and looked to her. She looked back, her expression shrewd and patient. For a moment Amy absolutely loved her friend, and the whole ordeal was slightly less terrifying, at least for half a second.

"You've met Shilling, ladies," Harry replied. "It absolutely hurts to talk to the ba—"

"Pick your next word very carefully, Pound," Amy warned.

The silence intensified. Laura was enthralled by the promise of scandal, and Jane looked ready to pull her out of the way the instant a fight might start. Harry cast his eyes down, grimacing politely.

"Of course," he said. "I apologise, that would have been most uncouth of me. You know me too well, Amy. The man brings out the worst in me."

"You condemn his ill manners, and surrender to your own," Amy criticised, folding her arms. "I mean it, Harry, at least Charlie is never malicious."

A vein in Harry's neck throbbed strenuously.

"I do apologise," he grated.

"And how long have we been calling Mister Shilling 'Charlie'?" Jane queried delicately.

"Daddy does it," Amy shrugged off nonchalantly,

confident that she'd heard him do it once at least, and watching carefully for Harry's pained reaction. His distress brought her no pleasure. She wanted to rewind time back to when everything had been normal, before these dark thoughts had rolled in and she had been forced to confront the concept that her entire life might be a lie. Unfortunately, that wasn't possible.

The sky was clouding over into what would almost certainly be another glorious sunset. The rain wouldn't hold off all night, but for now it was pleasant weather to be ruminating in. Charlie lay on the roof of the Pence building, staring at the sky, eating a pastry, and indulging in the aforementioned ruminating. Footsteps sounded behind him and he tilted his head further to look back. He got an upside-down view of two figures striding towards him. A short blonde man in white and a tall dark-haired man in black.

"You sent runners to say you wanted to see us?" Julian called as they strode towards him.

"If this is what I think it is, Sleuth, I'm throwing you off the roof," Mike added darkly.

"Don't get your knickers in a twist, Skipp," Charlie grinned, shoving the last of the pastry in his mouth. He rolled over and clambered to his feet. Quickly dusting off his hands, he rummaged in his pockets and pulled out some scraps of paper and a small cloth bag of trinkets. He handed them to Michael.

"Wait, really?" Michael raised an eyebrow, flicking quickly through the collection. "You did all of them?"

"The list wasn't that long," Charlie shrugged, voice muffled by pastry.

"You've been taking on extra cases?!" Julian exclaimed. "While the Jack is still at large?!"

"About that…" Charlie swallowed awkwardly and looked between his friends. "I needed to see you two. I need your help, but what I say here, now, it cannot leave this roof. It cannot be sold or bartered or passed on to another soul. I'm loathe to even speak of it to you… but I am wavering in indecision about what to do next."

"Do tell," Michael invited.

"You have our word we won't repeat it," Julian assured. "God herself knows you've earnt our trust."

Michael nodded in agreement. Charlie rubbed his mouth anxiously, trying to determine how to begin.

"I'm worried about Florin…" he started.

"Our good Doctor Amelia?" Julian smirked. Michael snorted. The two of them wore matching grins as they shared a glance.

"How very sweet of you, Charlie," Mike commented.

Charlie considered their expressions and body language. He sighed.

"Forget it," he shook his head. "You're both idiots."

"No, Sleuth, calm down," Julian bid him gently. "It's just so unlike you to show any interest in other people…"

"Starting with the boss' daughter-in-law does have a particularly 'you' flavour to it though," Michael added drily.

"She's in danger," Charlie insisted. "Possibly more than I initially realised. I'm trying to work out how to keep her out of harm's way, while still catching the Jack before he realises we're onto him."

"You actually think she's a target?" Julian checked. "She doesn't meet the criteria."

"She's an amalgamation of the criteria," Charlie sighed.

"She doesn't work for a High House," Julian countered.

"She—" Charlie stopped abruptly, pinching his lips together as the piece he'd been missing revealed itself to him. He cursed very silently in the back of his mind.

"You've just thought of something," Michael noted.

"It doesn't change the game," Charlie muttered. He drew closer and the other two huddled in. "This doesn't leave the rooftop," he whispered. They nodded. "The man from the park last night, the man all our evidence points to as the Jack of Hearts, is Henry Pound Junior, the Lord Chief Justice's son and Florin's betrothed."

"Jesus Christ," Julian cursed.

"If I didn't know you better, Charles, I'd say that was an incredibly bad taste joke," Michael grimaced. "She knows?"

"She worked it out and told me," Charlie admitted. "Now I need your help. If I tell you everything I know, will you help me keep her safe while we catch Pound Junior with enough evidence to put an end to these killings for good?"

# 12

The giant chandelier hung gleaming over the ballroom. People gathered together, talking, drinking, and dancing beneath its warm light. Servants bearing trays of canapés wound carefully between cliques of well-dressed party goers. Music and perfume filled the air.

Amy felt like she was walking through a nightmare. She didn't know how to tell anyone what was wrong, even though those closest to her kept asking. Otherwise, she fought to maintain her fake smile and forced jubilation. It was as exhausting as it was painful. Shilling had said he'd be here. He'd promised. There was still no sign of him. Had something happened? Was he all right?

She needed him here so that she could make him and Harry publicly compare wounds. Thanks to the papers, everyone knew Charlie had tangled with the Jack last night. Which meant that if she could get Jane and Laura to help her verify that Charlie and Harry had fought, then Harry was going to have some very public explaining to do.

He was standing across the room, talking with his friends. She couldn't help but notice that he hadn't turned his back on her all night. Whenever she looked for him, there he was, watching her. Part of her brain kept telling her that if someone she loved seemed to be going mad she would want to keep an eye on them too. He was just being protective. So why did it send nervous shivers up her spine? A hand touched her back. She jumped.

"I didn't mean to startle you, darling," Henry chuckled. "Pardon the intrusion, ladies." He looked around her current clique. Jane paused mid-joke, her eyes twinkling yet her expression deadpan.

"Not at all, my Lord, you are most welcome in our company," Laura beamed at him.

"Fair warning, Amy," Henry gave her a direct look from under his thick grey brows. "I wasn't the one who invited him tonight, and I'm not responsible for him."

"Charlie's here?" she exclaimed, ignoring the telling glances her friends shot her way.

Henry turned and waved someone from the doorway. Digby led a small troupe into the room, and Amy didn't bother to hide her surprise. They could almost have gone unnoticed… almost. Charlie strode in side-by-side with an impressively dapper Julian Silver, and the two men were flanked by a pair of uniformed officers. Heads turned as the police escorted the men into the room. Eyes caught Julian and stayed glued. Still, it was Charlie they started to whisper about. Amy could see it happening, like a match going off in a distillery. That was Charles Shilling, the man who had survived the Jack. What was he doing here? What was he doing with the police? She wanted to know the answer to that herself.

Charlie, for all that he was dressed up, still wore his shabby overcoat like he had fought the footman to keep it, and was his usual twitchy, harried self.

"Sorry we're late, Florin," he apologised. "This idiot took issue with my attire. We would have been much earlier if he wasn't so worried about clothes."

"Doctor Florin, congratulations," Julian kissed her hand. He was grinning openly at the situation. Amy could feel people around her swooning. She was confident it wasn't just her. He looked up at Henry. "My Lord Pound, you must be the proudest man in London tonight."

"Hello Julian," Amy smiled at him.

"So, you're the rogue who stole my daughter away in the middle of the night?" Henry grumbled. There was a notable shadow in his eyes as he beheld the man who looked like he could set off a dozen scandalous rumours just by breathing.

"The purest intentions only, my Lord, I assure you," Julian replied. "My friends had been gravely wounded, and Florin is possibly the only medic we know that Charlie here actually trusts."

"I got stabbed," Charlie admitted ruefully, touching the bandages beneath his waistcoat. "You remember Constables Wilson and Bond?" he gestured at the brunette man and blonde woman in uniform.

"I'm not sure we've met..." Amy said.

"Mister Shilling informed us that the case might be taking a dangerous turn for those investigating," Bond announced.

"Particularly for yourself, Doctor, and Mister Silver here," Wilson added. "Shilling has asked my partner and I to stand in as protection for you two, being as you are the medical specialist and unharmed key witness."

"I didn't realise we were considered to be in any danger," Amy tried to give Charlie a look.

"You can never be too careful, Florin," he shrugged in return. Charlie flipped open his satchel and removed a carefully wrapped object. "Julian was very clear about bringing a congratulatory gift."

"That's incredibly kind, but unnecessary," she replied.

"Humour us, Doctor," Julian smiled at her. "He's technically been a member of the aristocracy since Rebecca married, but we're still trying to teach him manners."

Charlie opened his mouth to start protesting and Julian glared warningly at him. Amy took the gift from him carefully as he handed it over like it was about to catch fire. As soon as the parcel left his hands, he stared Julian straight in the eye.

"Aristocracy is slavery," he began. "We should not be sustaining or celebrating a system designed to subjugate— *mguh*— *mffh*—!"

"So close," Julian sighed, grabbing Charlie from behind and clamping a hand over his mouth. "But what you meant to say was 'Congratulations, Doctor Florin. We couldn't be happier for you. Thank you for inviting us—' ow!" Charlie elbowed him in the ribs.

"How much does Susan Guinea pay you to mind him?" Jane asked curiously.

"What? Charlie?" Julian grinned. "Him I mind for free."

Several eyebrows shot up. Amy wondered if there was some ploy afoot to explain what Julian was doing here flirting with Charlie. Shilling wasn't known to do anything without a reason. She carefully unwrapped the item in her hands, realising what it was before she uncovered it. The beautiful rose vase from the mantlepiece that she had been admiring all morning.

"It was the only thing even vaguely appropriate that I knew you had any kind of fondness for," Charlie muttered, smoothing his coat again after being grabbed.

"You really didn't have to," she replied.

"That is stunning," Laura snuggled in close to her to admire the gift.

"Exquisite," Jane commented. "He might not like the aristocracy, but clearly likes their money."

Even hearing the words, Amy knew it wasn't true. Something didn't quite add up. Shilling wasn't the kind of person who would buy something like this, but he wouldn't steal a gift either. It puzzled her for a moment as she turned it in her fingers, until she brushed the backstamp on the bottom and tilted the vase to look. Etched in the clay was a small C.S. and a stamp of a cross. The ring. The same one that had marked Harry's cheek. The entire mantle of pottery suddenly made a surprising amount of sense.

"Charlie!" she exclaimed. "Did you make this?"

"Is that bad?" He froze awkwardly, glancing between her and Julian as though in trouble. Julian patted his shoulder reassuringly.

"No, Sleuth, you're doing great," he encouraged. "Man of many talents, our Charlie."

"Isn't he just," Henry commented slyly, as the doctors continued to inspect the vase.

"Good hobby..." Charlie muttered, fidgeting nervously. "Keeps the hands busy and the mind free. Rebecca's forbidden me from doing drugs in the house anymore. No more cough syrup. Not without doctors."

"And the real reason he's befriending our doctors comes out..." Harry drawled, arriving behind them. He strode up to the group casually, his expression as haughty as ever. Amy was struggling to reconcile how her closest companion had become a stranger so quickly. Once, she had found him handsome and charming. Now, he just looked arrogant.

"Hardly," Laura replied, still admiring the vase. "Access is not the issue, permission is. Besides, anyone who can make art like this can easily bribe any of the university doctors."

"I don't really need it," Charlie muttered. "It just alleviates the boredom when I'm between jobs. Helps me sleep. Easier just to stay busy." His anxiety seemed to slip as he met Harry's eye and curiosity got the better of him. "Wow, that looks worse in the light of day."

"If that's supposed to be an underhanded insult, Shilling, I assure you, even injured, my face still looks better than yours," Harry retorted.

"It wasn't," Charlie replied, oblivious to the insult. "I doubt you've met my friend, Julian Silver."

"I didn't know you had such expensive taste," Harry eyeballed Julian.

"Are you kidding?" Julian sized him up in return. "No one has to pay me to be here. If anything, I'd pay him."

"Julian can be rather protective," Charlie told everyone's surprised expressions. "He was with me last night, helped save Lizzie and myself, we might not have been so lucky without him. I don't think he has any intention of letting me go anywhere alone anymore."

"You must be the only person in the world who could sound disappointed at such company," Amy smiled.

"Well, perhaps someone can convince me you're in more danger than he is, and I could accompany you for the evening, Doctor," Julian flirted.

Amy felt her cheeks flush. She knew there was nothing behind his banter, that it was sweet but empty, and his intentions were nothing more than flattery. However, he was so handsome it wasn't fair that he was allowed to go around flirting with people.

"She's hardly in danger at her own party," Harry scoffed jealously. "And any danger she might be in, Shilling, is thanks to you and your investigation."

"Agree to disagree, Harry?" Charlie held out his hand. There was a challenge in his eyes and his stance. Harry met it without a flicker of hesitation. Anything less would have been failure. He clasped Shilling's hand firmly.

"With you? Always," he replied.

Charlie grasped Harry's arm warmly in both hands, squeezing congenially — right over his stitches. Harry hissed painfully, flinching away. Charlie didn't let him go. He stared Harry down, never breaking eye contact as he forced him to wince. Everyone saw.

"Whatever's wrong, Pound?" Julian queried. He feigned concern, but Amy could tell from the darkness in his eyes and the taunt in his tone that it wasn't sincere. Charlie had told him. Julian knew.

"Injury," Harry grated painfully.

"Poor Harry was mugged last night, would you believe," Laura announced, placing a gentle hand on his shoulder.

"You know, I actually wouldn't…" Charlie replied. He and Harry hadn't stopped staring at each other.

Amy felt her heart sink as any last shreds of doubt or hope that she had been clinging to faded away. Both men knew, with absolute certainty, that they had encountered each other last night, and both knew that the other knew too. Amy watched the realisation settle behind their eyes.

"It's no matter," Harry declared, his face pale and pinched as he carefully withdrew his arm. "You couldn't have known, Shilling. Unless you're about to do that ghastly party trick you do where you announce that my story must be false because I have the wrong kind of mud on my shoe?"

"I haven't been checking your shoes," Charlie replied. "But I could if you'd like? What were you wearing when you were out last night?"

The question hung damningly in the air. Amy felt her insides curl away from it.

"Honestly, I barely remember, and the servants will have cleaned them by now," Harry shrugged. "If you'll excuse me, I think I ought to check this."

"Take Mister Shilling with you," Jane suggested. Everyone stared at her. She met their surprise coolly and gave a direct nod to the gentlemen. "Amy has spoken of her theory that she believes the two of you may have been attacked by the same man last night. She said before that you should compare injuries. Why not now?"

"Brilliant, Jane!" Laura complimented her. "We could mediate, perhaps? Observant as our gentlemen are, medical professionals they are not."

"Not to mention their struggles with basic civility in each other's company," Jane smiled.

Amy watched her friends carefully. They both smiled politely at her. Polite, but knowing. They might not have known exactly what was going on, but they knew something was afoot, and they were stepping up to help. She wanted to grab them both and kiss them for their beautiful genius, but it was not the time. Instead, she settled for a grateful glance.

"A generous offer and an intriguing theory," Shilling conceded. "Perhaps we give Pound a moment to himself, before we descend on him in an investigative manner?"

"I hardly think that would be necessary, would it Harry?" Amy pressed. "It's just us, after all. The drawing room is right there."

Harry looked caught in a maelstrom. His eyes were tight, desperately trying to contain his panic. Charlie absentmindedly began to fidget with his ring, even though his face remained calm.

"Everyone should be allowed a minute to compose themselves before you drag them into another room and strip them down, Doctor," he advised.

She tried to glare at him, but he wouldn't meet her eye. Why was he ruining this? The plan was perfect. Her friends were helping, why was the detective sabotaging them?

"You know what she's like, Pound," Shilling nodded at him. "Never one to be dissuaded. You might as well take a moment while you can, and meet us in the drawing room when you're ready to be poked at by a small collection of beautiful women."

"Oh, the hardships of youth," Henry chuckled at them all.

Harry gave them a nod. He, too, looked wary. Charlie took him by the elbow and directed him away a few steps, whispering something. Harry murmured something back, his expression staying cautious, before pulling himself away and heading from the party. Amy wanted to hit them both over the head with a skillet. Charlie must have seen her anger when he turned back, but he shrugged at the group collectively.

"What? You think he's magically going to heal his injuries in the next five minutes?" he said.

"No one's criticising you, Charlie," Julian smiled. "We're just surprised."

"You're easily surprised for a man of your profession, Swift," Charlie grinned at him.

Something inside Amy snapped, watching them banter while she stood there, feeling like her entire life hung on a line. She handed the vase to Laura.

"Hold this a moment for me please," she requested, before snatching Charlie sharply by the arm. "I need to speak with Mister Shilling briefly. If you could all join us in the drawing room in a few minutes."

She ignored Charlie's pained protests as she gripped his arm tighter than was necessary.

"Amy—" Henry started.

"Not now, Daddy," she huffed, hauling Shilling from the room with her.

The others all watched them leave in confusion. Julian plucked a drink from a passing tray.

"I don't know which of them I'm more jealous of," he commented, sipping the drink. "Unsurprising though. Can't take him anywhere."

Amy kept a tight hold on her eccentric detective. She knew it didn't do to be so rough, especially given that he was injured, but she was too angry. Everything had lined up perfectly, and then Charlie had walked Harry right back out of it. She pulled him, wincing and yelping, into the drawing room with her. The room was still lit and the fire low from before the party. Henry's desk sat near a window curtained with heavy velvet drapes. Only once she had snapped the door shut behind them did she let Charlie go.

"What is the matter with you?!" she demanded. "We had him right there!"

"That's your plan?" Charlie rubbed his arm painfully. "Just get everyone to look at his injuries and what? My word against his? Julian's word? I'm not putting Swift in that position, Florin. I'm sorry. We need better than that."

"So you're just letting him go?" she hissed.

"Of course not!" Charlie replied. "I wouldn't put you in danger like that, Florin. No, I brought the officers with me tonight to help keep you safe. Julian came with me to help put the pressure on Harry. He knows that we know. Now, hopefully, he will have run as fast as he can to destroy any evidence he still has before we attempt to out him."

"And you're going to catch him in the act..." Amy caught on.

Charlie nodded. Amy bit her lip.

"That's not a completely stupid plan..." she conceded.

"Not completely," he agreed. "Can I ask you a personal question?"

His request hit her like a bucket of ice water. Panic gripped her and she felt herself chill to the bone. It shouldn't have been so intimidating, but it was him. He was standing so close again. It was like being caught in the doorway of his bedroom this morning all over again. She remembered how badly she hadn't wanted him to leave and how many times she had panicked in his absence since. He was going to ask her something she wasn't prepared to face, and under the sincerity of those patient grey eyes she wasn't going to be able to lie...

Still, curiosity got the better of her, and she nodded helplessly.

"Which High Houses did you look into signing up with a year ago?" Charlie asked.

Amy blinked at him. That wasn't what she'd been

expecting. How could he possibly—?

"Who told you?" she hissed.

He gave her a look. Of course. It was Charlie Shilling. No one had told him.

"It never got as far as proper negotiations," Amy muttered. "I only looked at a few places, and I don't know why it's any of your business. I just... I was going into my last year of study and I was struggling. My grades were still all right, mind you, but, just... emotionally, I was struggling. I was sick of medicine, and it helped a little to remember that I had options. Nothing had to be forever."

"Where and how long were you looking?" Charlie pressed.

"Both Mayfair Houses and one of the Kensington ones," she admitted reluctantly. "It wasn't for long. Knowing that I could throw it in for something else helped get me through. I didn't feel so trapped. Also, of course, then the killings started and..." she trailed off sickly, her hand leaping to her mouth as she realised what she was saying.

Charlie, of course, remained unsurprised. He'd already put the pieces together, which was why he knew she'd been looking.

"Oh my God..." she whispered behind her hand, horrified.

"If you're about to take this personally, Florin, don't," he advised gently. "You had no reason to believe all of this had anything to do with you, let alone find it centred on you, and unless you told Pound Junior to go out and murder those women, none of the blame falls on you."

"But it's my fault—" she choked.

"You cannot take responsibility for another's actions," Charlie insisted. "Not in this instance." He took her carefully by the shoulders as he continued to meet her eye. "I'm sorry, Florin. I really am, but I truly believe you are in more danger than I first realised. Please stay with the officers, with your father, with Julian — anyone that you are sure can keep you safe. I have to go after Harry before he actually manages to destroy any evidence."

"What are you going to do?" she asked.

"Whatever I have to," he shrugged. "Can't beat him in a fair fight, so I'll have to play a little unfair. Wish me luck?"

"Are you going to kill him?" she whispered in dread.

Charlie shook his head. "I don't want to kill anyone, not even over this."

Amy smiled. There were a lot of people who wouldn't blame him if he did. She knew part of the reason she'd asked was because she was one of them. Charlie wasn't like that. He didn't go for revenge. It was another one of the ways in which he was unusually good. In a spur of recklessness, she kissed his cheek as she wished him luck. It was worth it for the look of surprise on his face. He touched his face where her lips had pressed against his skin.

"Huh, not a bad plan," he mumbled. "Should have thought of it myself."

"Don't do anything stupid," she whispered, realising she hadn't moved away from him.

"No more than usual," he replied. Then he kissed her. The shock of the action was outweighed by the shock of realising that she was kissing him back. It was wildly inappropriate. It was wrong on so many levels. But his hand was warm against her cheek, and his lips were soft against hers, and she felt like she could just melt into his arms. He stayed close, his fingers still resting against her face as he whispered. "Very clever, Florin." Then, just as quickly, he was gone.

Amy stood, dumbstruck and breathless, as he dashed from the room. She felt dizzy. Her mind was so far up in the clouds it had overshot to the moon. Why did she do that? Why had he done that? At least no one had seen them. Still, as deeply as she knew she shouldn't have done it, she could hear a small voice in the back of her head warn her that didn't mean she wouldn't do it again.

# 13

Charlie hurried up the stairs, moving as quickly and quietly as he could. The lipstick was a stroke of genius. He never would have thought of it himself. She was really very clever, that Doctor Florin. Still, she had the benefit of advanced social and medical knowledge, an excellent education, and strong emotional intelligence — the combination of which had made her admirably logical. He had considered himself equally rational, until several seconds ago. The plan was so clever, he hadn't accounted for the fact that kissing her might addle his brain a little, and had consequently almost run into a doorframe.

Now was not the time for his brain to betray him like that. He needed his brain. He was going after Harry Pound. He was stalking the Jack of Hearts.

Sure enough, he heard the crime before he saw it. The layout of the Pounds' house was easy enough to deduce. Everyone else was busy downstairs. Charlie had expected to find Harry in his bedroom, but his personal study made just as much sense. The door hadn't quite shut behind him, and Charlie could see the firelight from the hearth through the crack. He could hear the clink of glass and the strained grunt of exertion.

He pushed the door further with his foot.

Harry froze. He was bent over a large wooden chest that had been half-pulled out from the wall, previously wedged between a bookcase and the door. The flat top of it looked like it had been used as a side table for the reading chairs positioned in the corner by the bookcases. The other side of the room was home to a large desk, right in front of the fire.

"You're not allowed up here," Harry grated, looking up at him from where he hauled at the chest.

"I guess we're both doing a lot of things we're not allowed to do at the moment, then," Charlie replied. "What's in the box?"

"Get out of here, Shilling," Harry ordered, letting go and standing straight. They both stood a moment, eyeing each other up. "Leave now, walk away from this house, and don't ever come back. Final warning."

"Or what?" Charlie asked.

"Or your ghost will be stuck with a lot of regret," Harry threatened.

Charlie smiled at the threat. Harry really had a way with words when it came to him. It felt deeply personal. Hopefully this would too. He pushed the door the rest of the way open and stepped inside. The light in the room was better than it had been in the hallway. They faced each other across the chest.

"And to think the world keeps trying to tell me you're a smart man..." Harry drawled.

"I've caught you, Harry," Charlie shrugged. "All theories of possible motive disturb me deeply, but we both know you were the man I met in the park last night."

"You didn't win that fight then, Shilling. What makes you think you'll win it now?" Harry taunted.

"I don't have to win. I just have to protect Florin," Charlie replied. He touched his lip nervously. It was possibly a bit much, but he wanted to make sure Harry noticed. It worked.

Amy was still standing in a daze in the drawing room when the others trailed in. Henry led them forcefully, flanked by Wilson and Bond, with Jane just behind, dragging Laura and Julian in her wake. They looked like they meant business. Amy just wished she didn't feel quite so dizzy.

"All right, Amy," Henry huffed, sweeping into the room. "What in God's name is going on? Heaven knows I've been patient, but something is afoot and I demand to know what! Hm? What was all that business with Harry and Shilling out there?"

"Where is Shilling?" Julian added curiously, swirling his glass. "You didn't throw him out a window, did you? Not that you'd be the first, but I hate having to explain it to Rebecca."

"She's the Jack!" Wilson pointed. "She threw Shilling out the window!"

"No one threw Shilling out a window," Amy said exasperatedly, as Bond carefully lowered her partner's accusatory finger.

"If you sent him upstairs to help undress Harry, I still think we should supervise," Laura offered cheekily.

"Enough joking," Henry snapped. "Please, everyone. I feel like I'm five steps behind on something. Amy, darling, what is going on with Shilling and Harry? This all seems like I've wandered into one of your horrendous novels." His thick brows were so stern, but his eyes were patient with determination.

Amy met his eye and she swore she could feel the exact moment her heart finally broke. She couldn't tell him. She still couldn't tell him, not even as sure as she was now. She couldn't be the one to say it. Those serious brown eyes were Harry's eyes. She couldn't tell him that his son was a killer. She just couldn't. She put a hand to her lips and turned away. If she looked at him a moment longer, she was going to burst into tears. There was a chance she still might.

"Amy, whatever it is, you can tell us," Henry pleaded.

"Does it have anything to do with the odd duck… and the way you seem to be looking at it like you think it might be a gosling…?" Jane asked leadingly.

Amy rolled her eyes and prayed for calm. She was going to have to say something eventually. Was it going to be worse to admit she'd kissed Charlie than it would be to try and tell them Harry was the mystery attacker from the park? The Jack himself. Then she remembered… she wasn't the only one who knew. Even as she thought it, Julian sidled up beside her. He gave her a look over the rim of his glass, then subtly touched the corner of his mouth.

"Do you have a handkerchief on you, Doctor?" he whispered. "Your lipstick is ever so slightly smudged..."

Amy took her fingers from her lips. They were lightly stained with a deep red. The penny dropped. She cursed so violently that everyone else startled. Cries of disapproval went completely ignored as Amy leapt to her father's desk. She ripped open the drawer and grabbed his pistol.

"Amy!" Henry bellowed at her.

"He's going to get himself killed!" she yelled back, clutching the gun in one hand, hoisting her skirts in the other, and bolting for the stairs.

Harry's expression flattened when he saw the lipstick, like a bull seeing red. Charlie had less than a second to be pleased about the success of his provocation. He jumped away as Harry leapt over the chest. Harry's long arms snatched for the back of his coat. His fingers clawed across Charlie's back but didn't catch him. Charlie threw himself over the desk, trying to put distance and cover between them. He muffled a cry as something horrible happened to his stitches. The rug by the fire cushioned his knees as he hit the floor.

Charlie grabbed the poker by the fire. He scrambled painfully to his feet, holding his side, and swung the poker as Harry charged him. Harry caught it. His fist closed around the metal spike, stopping it dead. Charlie had a whole second to realise his mistake. Then the poker was ripped from his hands. He staggered and hunched, trying to shield himself and back away.

The poker struck the back of his shoulder. Twice. He heard something crack. The pain each time was a blinding flare. He didn't know what had broken. He stumbled around the desk, trying to feel his way. He was bleeding through his shirt again.

Harry grabbed him. Charlie shoved him away. Everything hurt. The pain flared and he whimpered. Harry caught him again, still so much bigger and stronger than Charlie. Charlie felt a curtain cord loop around his neck. He struggled and panicked, grabbing the rope with both hands and leaving his side to bleed. The cord tightened. His fingers were barely holding it back. He started to choke.

"Just think..." Harry hissed in his ear, "what will everyone say when they find your body and discover you were the Jack all along?"

Charlie struggled, gasping. He twisted and pulled at the cord, his eyes watering, blood seeping from his side.

"When they find you guilt-ridden, hanging above all your trophies..." Harry continued. "In the secret little space you'd been hiding your kills."

"No... one... will... believe..." Charlie choked, fighting against the rope.

"Oh, they will," Harry assured. "The evidence will be overwhelming."

"Set... up..." Charlie slumped over the desk, reaching out desperately. He grabbed a paperweight and swung it back, smashing it over Harry. The cord loosened. Charlie threw himself clear, hitting the floor on his hands and knees. He coughed desperately. "No one will believe you, Harry!" he yelled, crawling away weakly. "I have indisputable alibis for half the killings. The police know I'm not doing it. They will know it's a set up. Everyone will know."

Charlie pulled himself towards the doorway, trying to stagger to his feet. His knees were shaking and his head was spinning. His lungs hurt. Hands grabbed him again, lifting him off the ground from behind. A knife pressed against his throat.

"Fine!" Harry retorted. "Then I guess you'll just have to be the Jack's latest victim, and you can serve as a warning, Shilling! Believe me, when they find you... the world will get to see what happens to a filthy rat when it thinks it can take on a lion."

"HARRY!"

The door burst open so hard it hit the wall. Amy stood, gun raised, with a small crowd of horrified onlookers. Her cheeks were flushed, her chest heaving, her curls escaping around her face, but her hands were steady and her eyes fierce.

"Harry, drop him!" she bellowed.

Charlie felt like he was going to faint. His throat his hurt and everything was spinning. Florin looked like an avenging angel in the doorway, gowned in flaming red. He'd really expected this to go better.

"This isn't what it looks like," Harry defended. "He's trying to frame me! He's trying to steal Amy!"

"No he isn't, Harry," she disagreed. "We heard you when we were coming up the corridor. We heard everything. Put him down before this gets any worse."

Harry's grip tightened on Charlie, pulling him in and pressing the blade hard enough to draw blood.

"You kissed him..." he accused.

"We smeared some lipstick on him to provoke you," Amy snarled. "All too easy, I might add." She paused a moment, and Charlie heard the catch in her voice when she spoke again, the slight tremor. "Why, Harry?" she begged. "Why did you do it? All those women... what in Hell could have possessed you?"

"It wasn't me!" Harry lied, but Charlie could hear real panic in the voice by his ear now. "He's lying! He's been lying to you, Amy! He's trying to turn you against me! You know I would never—! If you hadn't been trying to help him—"

"Bullshit, Harry!" she yelled, still holding the gun on him. "I wasn't helping him; he was helping me. Charlie didn't catch you. I did. I went to him last night because I worked it out. I put the pieces together. You came to me, Harry, to me, with those injuries — like I wouldn't notice — like I wouldn't smell the formaldehyde with the blood, or see the glue on your lip, or the bruise from Charlie's ring!"

"Amy..." Harry breathed.

Charlie snatched the knife. He took his chance and grabbed Harry's hand, pulling the blade away from his throat. They struggled. Charlie elbowed Harry sharply in the gut. Harry grunted. Charlie managed to rip himself free. He hit the floor again, desperately trying to roll away. Multiple people were yelling. Bodies swarmed above him. Hands grabbed him, pulling him back from danger. Then a new voice cut through the chaos.

"ENOUGH!" Lord Pound bellowed.

Charlie struggled onto his elbows. He was bleeding onto the carpet, but none of it seemed fatal. Julian was holding him gently, trying not to make the situation worse, but keeping him out of mortal peril. Constables Wilson and Bond had Harry disarmed and pinned to the floor.

Everyone froze at the sound of Lord Pound losing his temper. He stood in the doorway, his face pale and tight, and looked down on the chaos below him. Amy looked equally distraught at his side as he reached out a hand and carefully took the gun off her.

"Doctors," he glanced back at Jane and Laura. "Please tend to Mister Shilling before he does himself some permanent damage."

They nodded, but didn't move into the room until he did. Henry bid Amy stay in the doorway with a gesture as he entered the room and crossed to the chest. Jane and Laura followed him in silently and knelt beside Charlie, taking him carefully from Julian's arms as they started checking him over and applying pressure to his wounds. Henry reached for the lid.

"Father! Don't!" Harry cried, struggling against the police. "It's a set up!"

Henry had the look of a man who had already heard too much, and wasn't prepared to listen to much else. He clicked the latch and opened the chest. It was full of old robes and paperwork, but the scent was as old and rotten as it was chemical. It wafted into the room like toxic smoke. He reached in and pulled some of the robes aside. A small, battered diary fell out. Glass bottles clinked. Henry carefully pulled one out. Suspended in a tightly sealed jar of liquid was what looked suspiciously like a human heart. There were more jars in the chest. A lot more.

No one said anything. Amy had started to cry silently. Tears were pouring down her cheeks and both hands covered her mouth. Henry wouldn't look at his son. He stood by the chest, the one person with the best view of the contents, frozen like a statue. Finally, in a deadly soft tone, he spoke over the crackling fire.

"Constables, take the Jack down to holding and keep multiple guards on him at all times."

"Yes Sir," they replied, cuffing Harry's hands behind his back and hauling him to his feet.

"Father—!" Harry protested.

"Get him out of my sight!" Henry bellowed, refusing to look at him. "And do not let him speak to anyone!" He carefully placed the jar back into the chest and moved to pull Amy safely out of the doorway. She curled into his arms, burying her face in his chest and sobbing as Harry was dragged from the room. Henry kept his attention on her, holding her close, his expression downcast and grief-stricken.

Silence reigned in the aftermath as everyone tried to process what had happened. Charlie sat on the floor, trembling as the doctors checked him over.

"You're going to need new stitches," Jane told him softly.

They all looked to Amy, weeping in Henry's arms. It

didn't seem right to interrupt, but they needed something. Laura got to her feet and headed for the door.

"I'll go ask downstairs," she told them. "Someone will have something."

"My medical bag is in my room!" Amy exclaimed, turning. Her face was drenched with tears and she could barely look at them, her hands lingering at her cheeks. "It's just down the hall."

"Come with us, Doctor Mark," Henry sighed. "We'll find you what you need."

She nodded her thanks as they moved to leave.

"Wait!" Charlie lurched off the floor. Everything pulled and he stumbled, blood dripping onto the ground. The wince was impossible to keep back. He felt like he might faint, but he had to say something. "I'm sorry," he apologised, trying to meet Amy and Henry's eyes. "I am, truly, so sorry… I didn't mean for this —"

"Not now, Shilling," Henry shook his head. "Not now."

Julian stood and caught Charlie by the arm, keeping him upright as Henry guided Amy and Laura from the room. Charlie grimaced painfully, leaning on his friend as Jane motioned him to sit their distracted patient back on the floor.

"I… I was just trying…" Charlie muttered.

"We know, Sleuth," Julian kissed the top of his head and sat him back down. "We know. You did good."

# 14

The next morning, Charlie woke in his own bed. It was soft and warm, and he was on enough drugs for the pain that for a moment everything felt wonderful, until he tried to roll over. Reality hit him extremely painfully from multiple angles. His side burned, the back of his shoulder seared, and his throat was definitely bruised. He lay pitifully on his side and buried his face in his pillow. It was full of the scent of Florin's perfume. His chest hurt.

The memories of the night before were a confused and agonised jumble in his head. He was going to need a whole pot of tea to help organise them, and some bread. Bread meant getting up. Bread meant finding pants. He deliberated on it for some time, and then decided it was worth it.

He had managed to get out of bed and was almost completely dressed when his bedroom door opened. Rebecca took one look at him, struggling to pull his injured body into his waistcoat (the shirt had been a feat of absolute triumph), and she sighed.

"What are you doing out of bed, Charlie?" she asked.

"Bread," he grunted, trying to bend his injured

shoulder back.

"I can have someone bring you breakfast," she reminded, crossing the room to help him.

"Servitude is subjugation and I will not be a part of it," he grumbled.

"It's their job, Charlie, they get paid for it," Rebecca said, helping to tug him into his clothes. "Besides, you're injured. If you were confined to your bed, you wouldn't have any problem with me hiring a nurse to help care for you, would you?"

"But that isn't why someone would bring me food, is it?" Charlie argued. "It's not because I need care, it's because your rich wife encourages a crippling and divisive class system, which forces people into poverty and keeps them enslaved to those with power in order to meet their most basic needs."

"Do you want to tell her that?" Becky raised an eyebrow.

"Not really…" Charlie muttered. He'd had that fight with Susan before, and while he was still absolutely sure he was right, she was very scary. "Becky, please, just help me get my coat on and then I can set the kettle for tea before I go to the bakery."

"How about you go to the bakery," she suggested, pulling him into his coat, "and I'll make you a pot of tea for when you get back?"

Charlie considered this. "I'm not sure I trust you not to get one of the servants to make it while I'm gone…" he mused.

"I wouldn't do that to you, Charlie," she smiled. "Not today. You more than earnt a day off after last night. Go see Mike, and I'll make you some tea."

It seemed an adequate agreement, and he shuffled his way to the front door. His legs were fine, after all, and he was very capable of walking himself across the road. It was just everything above his waist he had to be careful of as he travelled. He wrapped his scarf very gently and carefully over his bruises and stepped out into the world.

Terry saw him coming from the front counter and motioned him around the back before he even made it inside. Charlie gave him a nod and staggered around to the alley. Mike was already waiting for him. He dragged a wooden crate over, patted the top of it, and held out a buttery knot. Charlie sank down gratefully, attacking the crusty bread like a sleepy puppy.

"You missed the horde of photographers outside your house this morning," Michael commented.

"*Hgh?*" Charlie responded, mouth full.

"Jasper chased them off," Mike smiled.

"That doesn't sound like something Jasper would do," Charlie replied. "He's bloody allied with journalists in the past."

"Yes, but he will do absolutely anything Lady Guinea asks of him," Michael pointed out. "Including emptying chamber pots onto unsuspecting loiterers trying to snap your picture."

Charlie grimaced at the notion. "So the news is out there, then? I'm surprised anyone cares about me today."

"Granted, most people will be hounding the Pound residence," Mike agreed. "But the papers do say you caught him. Full credit."

"But Florin…?" Charlie protested.

"If you can get me inside information on what's happening with your new doctor, I'd be grateful," Mike gave him a look. "Everything's very hush there."

Charlie returned the look. Where Mike's was inquiring, Charlie's was warning and powerfully unrelenting. He wasn't going to spy on Florin, not even for Mike. His friend gave him a nod.

"I presume you got a detailed account from Swift?" Charlie asked.

"He was extremely generous with the specifics and— no! Will you shut up?!" Mike snapped at the mischievous grin Charlie directed his way. Charlie remained silent and there was no need to point out that he hadn't said anything. "Swift told me what happened last night. As per usual, the papers had the entire event before I could do anything with it. I'm not really trying though. Your adventures have been a bit too high-profile recently. I just like to stay abreast of it all, on a personal level— Christ, Charlie, will you shut up?! How are you even making something out of that?!"

Charlie said nothing. He ripped a small nugget of bread from the knot and popped it innocently in his mouth. His eyes were managing to hold an entire insinuating conversation on their own.

"I'm surprised Pound didn't kill you last night," Michael muttered.

"He gave it his best shot," Charlie replied, unwinding his scarf and exposing his bruises. Mike flinched at the sight of them.

"Oh God... Charlie..." Mike crouched down and touched his arm, meeting his eye. "Heavens, I'm sorry, I... I shouldn't joke..."

"It's fine, Skipp," Charlie smiled at him. "If you weren't being waspish I'd worry something was wrong with you." He shoved the last of the bread in his mouth, chewed and swallowed, and then held his hand out. "I'm going to need another three of those, a pastry, and the list of jobs you've got in your pocket."

"What?" Mike responded.

"Cough it up, bread-boy," Charlie grinned.

"I'll grab you the baking, but I don't have a list," Mike lied, standing up again.

"Yes, you do," Charlie disagreed. "I wasn't sure, but I noticed you decide not to give it to me when you saw my neck. Did Swift tell you about the rest of it?"

"Yeah, he did," Mike admitted. "But you know what he's like. Can be a bit dramatic at times."

"He likes to think of it as passionate," Charlie smirked.

"Shut it, Sleuth," Mike warned. "Your body might be bruised, but your brain ought to know better."

Charlie held out his hand more insistently. Mike sighed.

"I'm not giving you work to do when you're injured," he argued. "Julian and Rebecca would kill me."

"What they don't know won't hurt them," Charlie replied. "Besides... Becky is getting Jasper to brew tea... I know... I can feel it... so we owe her no loyalty. The Jack is in custody. I guess it's just business as usual."

"Already?" Mike questioned dubiously.

"No reason not to," Charlie assured.

Mike looked like he was looking for an excuse to disagree, but coming up short in the face of Charlie's insistence. He sighed and reached into the pocket of his apron, pulling out a grubby scrap of paper and handing it over.

"There's only a couple of things, but don't tell Swift I gave them to you," he ordered. "I'll go grab you an order to go."

Michael stalked back inside. Charlie unfolded the list and ran his eyes over the scrawled details. Easy. He'd have them both done by the end of the day. Business as usual indeed.

Thus concludes *The Jack of Hearts Murders* Book One of the *Shilling & Florin Mysteries*. The story continues in
BOOK TWO:
THE THIEF & THE MARQUIS

Did you enjoy this book?

Please consider leaving a review for it on Amazon or Goodreads. Every positive review allows me to spend more time writing books for you to enjoy!

# OTHER BOOKS BY KATE HALEY

Welcome to the Inbetween

The Light After Earth

Like the Heroes of Old

## Shilling & Florin Mysteries

1. The Jack of Hearts Murders

2. The Thief & the Marquis

3. A Dalliance with Grief

4. The Case of Silver & Sovereign

5. A Cold & Bitter Revenge

6. The Pen & the Blade

7. Blood & Bells

8. Tarnished Silver

## The War of the North Saga

Footsteps into the Unfamiliar (short story collection)

1. Steel & Stone

2. Magic in the Marshes

3. Forest of Ghosts

4. Women of the Woods

5. Spirit & Sand

6. The Prince and the Witch

7. Gods & Dragons

## The Vincent Temple Trilogy (+ Prequel)

Path of Dreaming Souls (Prequel)

1. Gateway to Dark Stars

2. Tomb of Endless Night

3. Fortress of the Shadow Reich

# ABOUT THE AUTHOR

Kate Haley is a speculative fiction author who works predominantly in fantasy and horror.

While currently content to fill their days with writing and table-top RPGs, their grander plans involve world domination. Something akin to the tyranny of the greatest city atop the Disc would be an acceptable standard. They believe a super-villainous overlord would be an upgrade, given that our current villains lack style and imagination.

After all, super-villainy requires Presentation.

If you like their references, consider visiting their website www.katehaleyauthor.com for short fictions and merchandise, and join the mailing list for early access and exclusive cool stuff.

You can also get in touch through the website regarding their work, your position in future slave armies, or a general interest in all things nerdy and wonderful.

Printed in Dunstable, United Kingdom